MEGAN NOLAN

Megan Nolan was born in 1990 in Waterford, Ireland, and is currently based in New York. Her essays and reviews have been published by the *New York Times*, *White Review*, *Guardian* and *Frieze* amongst others. For her debut novel, *Acts of Desperation*, Nolan was the recipient of a Betty Trask Award, shortlisted for the *Sunday Times* Young Writer of the Year Award and longlisted for the Dylan Thomas Prize.

T0322200

ALSO BY MEGAN NOLAN

Acts of Desperation

MEGAN NOLAN

Ordinary
Human Failings

VINTAGE

5 7 9 10 8 6 4

Vintage is part of the Penguin Random House group of companies
whose addresses can be found at global.penguinrandomhouse.com

Penguin
Random House
UK

First published in Vintage with new material in 2024
First published in hardback by Jonathan Cape in 2023

Copyright © Megan Nolan 2023, 2024

penguin.co.uk/vintage

Printed and bound in Great Britain by Clays Ltd, Elcograf S.p.A.

The authorised representative in the EEA is Penguin Random House Ireland,
Morrison Chambers, 32 Nassau Street, Dublin D02 YH68

A CIP catalogue record for this book is available from the British Library

ISBN 9781529922639

Penguin Random House is committed to a sustainable future
for our business, our readers and our planet. This book is made
from Forest Stewardship Council® certified paper.

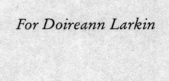

For Doireann Larkin

Part I

Down below in Skyler Square the trouble was passing quickly from door to door, mothers telling mothers, not speaking aloud but somehow saying: *baby gone, bad man, wild animal.*

*

1.
CARMEL

The night the child went missing, Carmel sat a few miles away in the window of a cafe in Brockley. She was breathing hard, cloud on the glass. Passing by, a man glanced in to check her prettiness and was struck by the intensity of her face behind the patch of steam which partially obscured it. She ignored the gentle rattle of plates and hiss of chips which went on behind her, hearing nothing. When she let herself pore over memories, she was hawkish. Filled with greed for one of the only pleasures remaining to her, raking through lost evenings and moments. It was rare that she did allow herself this. It had been so long that she knew there could only be a handful more times. It would not always be possible to summon precisely the fast-fading textures and tastes.

When the child was missing, while the courtyard was lighting up with drama and anguish, Carmel was thinking about sex. She tried to mete out the different encounters they had shared together and not think of them all at once as a conflated interaction, not to waste her thoughts in an incoherent wave. Rather she had separated them out years ago and given them titles and would think of them only with great care. Often, because her and Derek's affair had taken place almost exclusively in the privacy of his apartment, they were called after things they had consumed together, and which she could then recall the taste of in his mouth.

Particular drinks (White Russian Night), plain meals he had cooked with sweet incompetence (Spaghetti Bolognese Night), takeaway pizza with a faint cardboard flavour (Gino's Night). Most often what she tasted was the familiar paternal smell of beer and cigarettes on his moustache, a beautiful acrid dream sense which haunted her. Other nights were named after a book he had been reading at the time (*Of Human Bondage* Night), or a chapter she had been studying ('Home Rule' Night). She could see with perfect clarity the books being laid aside when they became too impatient.

The clothes she had worn were another method, to think of him undoing the side clasp of a kilt, or pulling up the snug wool jumper she had stolen from her brother after he had shrunk it in the wash. There were ways to do it, ways to differentiate. Despite what had resulted, and what they had meant for the rest of her life, their nights together had not been so many. They weren't enough that the ways he touched or looked at her were easily muddled together.

These too were divisible, the disbelieving ecstasy on his face when she first parted her legs and let him see her with light, without shame. The confusing joy of him slipping a finger inside her mouth, gently probing so that she felt evaluated like a body, like an animal, but happily. And now, in her window haze, she let herself murmur his name to herself as she almost never did and felt for a moment the fervent rise of devotion which used to be so constant. The feeling, which she knew was also a lie, that she would do anything for him, anything to have him again for a minute. To confirm that his sweat smelled that way it did in her mind, so green and pleasant. If it had been true, if she would have done anything to get him back, then she would have done it at the time. She would have done the one thing guaranteed to summon him when he left.

She was allowing herself the indulgence of memory because her second remaining pleasure, that of sleep, had been torn from her that morning. It was strange that sleep had come to mean so much. She resisted it for most of her life. As a young person she found it a darkly boring prospect, all that waste of fun and thought, and as an adult was fearful that its oblivion was too close to death, too tempting to trust as an indulgence. Later she accepted its blankness as positive, when she stopped believing in the chance of positive movement and embraced distraction as the only possible relief.

There were two nights, soon after her mother had died, when she left the flat.

I'll be gone for two days, she told her father and brother, You can look after Lucy for two days?

Her father wanted to ask what she was doing but didn't. Her brother nodded. The child would be taken care of. She used money she had saved to book two nights in a hotel in Little Venice, somewhere a woman who worked in the shop had gone for her anniversary. She wasn't sure what she was doing exactly but felt that if there was any time to lose herself in new sex it was now, in the mud of grief. She packed a bag with her least-frayed underwear and her best dresses and walked the few hours to the hotel. After throwing her bag in the room, surprisingly shabby and insect-ridden, she showered and did herself up and went down to the bar. She assumed something happened in hotel bars, that was the received wisdom.

After two drinks, and one unappealing pissed businessman,

she ventured out. She had three more drinks at three different pubs, hoping for something. It seemed impossible that it wouldn't take place. Some of them looked at her, but nobody approached, nobody even nodded hello in a promising way. Back in her room she found a long foreign hair in the sheets, and more insects in the bath. She stamped her foot in disappointed rage, shouted oh fuck you at a broken window latch which wouldn't allow any air in. She checked the rest of the bed for stray foreign bodies, found one more hair which was different to the first, and started laughing. She got into the bed with it, drunk, resigned to disgust and disappointment. She thought about how she would sometimes find Derek's hairs inside her own underwear the next day and how unspeakably thrilling it was. She would press them against her lower belly as though they could put him back inside of her, that pure agony, how deep the ache in her lowest body was, pain that could only be resolved by the return of its cause.

That night in the hotel her disillusion was so great that she accepted the weight of sleep she had formerly resisted. She slept for twelve hours and rose and ate an early dinner on Formosa Street, a big bowl of spaghetti, then returned immediately to sleep, which had become delicious. When she was roused from it by the cooing of birds at the window she cursed them and went immediately back into it. She had learned there was one more love in her life, this kind of disappearance.

In the cafe in Brockley, pushed out of her sexual reveries by the owner, a kind woman called Sally, closing up, she thought again how deprived she had been that morning. She had been in a perfect sleep, dreaming of an enormous cinema and the feeling of slyly touching hands, when Lucy had run in and screamed that everyone was down in the courtyard playing a game and could she go too.

Yes, yes, Carmel said, go on.

2.
TOM

Tom stared at himself in the lift mirror as it trundled down, lit with a brutal glare. He shook his head, loosening the hair and then raking it backwards. He exhaled a long slow sigh and let his lips stay stuck out as it whistled to an end. He held the pout for a moment, squinting, then laughed nervously and stuck his tongue out, making a brief retching sound before readjusting himself back to the mannered, carefully casual stance he maintained while out on a job.

He wore a Fruit of the Loom faded sweatshirt and black Levi's. His boss Edward had burst out laughing the first time he had seen this outfit on Tom.

Are you doing a little performance as an Everyman, Hargreaves? he said.

Tom had flushed at this even as he laughed along. There was nothing he wanted more than Edward's approval, he had learned to live for the brief ecstasy of a Good work, lad, or a Knew I could count on you.

Afterwards he felt aggrieved and defensive, bickering with him inside his head. These were the clothes he had worn in Margate before he moved to London and started working for the papers. They were the clothes of normal people, it was only that he'd been playing at being one of the others for long enough that a return to his old home stuff looked comical and perverse.

Peasants, that was what Edward and the others (barring a few hand-wringing employees who were biding their time to make a break for one of the leftie rags) called everyone who was not a journalist or royalty or a celebrity. Peasants were the cheapo hookers who'd had it off with footballers getting paid a few hundred quid for a tell-all, peasants were single mothers with hyperactive children whom they could sell as the NEIGHBOURS FROM HELL. Peasants were small-scale drug dealers who worked in public-facing jobs.

(Tom's first story in a national was about a school-crossing guard who sold pills to primary school children when he came off his shift. He'd never existed, of course, Anto the lollipop drug lord was Tom's flatmate Harry with his back to the camera, dressed up in a big beefy tracksuit with a neon vest over it, his shaven head buffed to gleam a little more threateningly.)

Peasants were crooks, bin-men whinging over wages, alcoholics, churchgoing Holy Joes, old people ringing in complaining about telly storylines, slappers, nurses, bouncers on the make, but most importantly, most of all, peasants were the readers.

In the lift mirror he checked himself one more time before exiting to go and have a walk round the square and see what he could gather about the families.

Meeting his own eyes for a moment he had one of the jarring intrusive thoughts which he had, quite often, to suppress lately. Mostly they came when he was trying to sleep, if he had not drunk enough alcohol to make it instantaneous. But they came also during the morning news editorial meetings, particularly when he was being inadequate and panicking about it, failing to light up Edward's eyes with anything juicy, feeling the ever-present danger of an imminent bollocking. The thoughts got there first, belting out 'Fucking cunt stupid cunt' with such an alarming urgency he had to fight the impulse to laugh or cry out. They sometimes had an almost jubilant quality, like a quick burst of circus music being blared at overwhelming volume right inside his skull.

I'm the loneliest man in the world, this one in the lift screamed as he regarded himself, *I'm the loneliest man in the world!*

*

TERROR IN NUNHEAD AS BODY OF MISSING INFANT DISCOVERED NEXT TO BINS
By Tom Hargreaves

Residents of the Skyler Square housing estate were reeling early this morning after the body of three-year-old Mia Enright was found after a night of agonised searching. Devastated neighbours who discovered Mia reported that she appeared to have bruising around her neck, spurring speculation that she had been deliberately injured.

Charles and Etta Enright, a popular young couple who friends say are a community staple helping to run youth clubs and activities for unemployed adults in the area, were today being comforted by relatives. Mia was last seen in the communal courtyard of her estate playing with her older brother, Elliott, along with other neighbourhood children. She was assumed to have wandered off and become lost, initiating a huge search effort, before tragically being found dead just a few hundred feet from where she had disappeared.

Brian Edwards, Etta's brother, released a short statement on behalf of the family which read: 'Mia brought immeasurable joy to our entire family with her infectious laughter and dazzling spirit. She enjoyed every moment of her short time on this earth and it is this we will remember while we try to find the strength to endure the grief we now face. My family ask for privacy at this time.'

3.

Tom heard of the disappearance of Mia Enright before any other hack through pure luck. He was having a drink with a waitress, Ruth, he had picked up a few weeks back near the Millwall football stadium. He had friends in the area and occasionally hung about on volatile match days in case something interesting happened. The waitress suggested they go back to her place. Her mum was away, the place was empty. The mention of a mum gave Tom brief pause, but he scrutinised the faint crow's feet barely visible beneath the make-up and judged the situation to be tolerable. She was twenty at least and even if she wasn't quite, he was only twenty-eight himself, it was hardly like he was a dirty old man, ha ha ha.

By the time they'd made their way back to Skyler Square Mia had been missing for several hours and the central courtyard was buzzing with throngs of neighbours, the ones too old or infirm or indifferent to help search. The waitress took his hand and led him right into the heart of the chatter, trying to find out what was going on. Before he even heard what it was that had taken place, he was feeling more relaxed than he had all day.

He bristled in the excitable anxiety, almost smelling it. He knew something fruitful, something potentially magnificent, had fallen into his lap.

I need to use your phone, he said to Ruth, the pretence of dreamy amiability he usually affected with women gone in a moment.

But she hadn't a phone she told him, her mum didn't like them, she had nerves and when phones rang they made her panic. Why do you need a phone? she asked him, and he quickly calculated how the next few hours might proceed.

Because, he said, I've got an uncle in Camberwell and I want to let him know to spread the word down there in case nobody knows yet.

Her eyes softened a little at this, as intended, and he said to her, I'm going to go and find a phone box, Ruth, and let Uncle Michael know.

Even as he said this he had to restrain himself from exploding with artifice, Uncle Michael, Uncle fucking Michael!

But will you do me a favour? Will you let me come back and stay with you tonight? I don't mean like that, not now, I just want to be here to help look for Mia and do anything I can.

He cocked his head beseechingly to the side, eyes large and soulful, full of sorrowful determination, and what was amazing was that in the moment there was even some part of him that believed what he was saying, believed that what he was going to do was for Mia. *Baby Mia*, he thought to himself, *Baby Mia will play*.

*

On the phone to Edward he said it might come to nothing but it might be a big one – tiny kid missing, someone had shown him a picture, blonde hair in pigtails, big blue eyes, those slightly heartbreaking pink plastic glasses they do for babies, devastating grin. Her family are saints apparently, every one of the neighbours falling over themselves to say how decent they are, even the really sour-faced old biddies, they've sort of turned the estate around, used to be druggies and alkies on the stairwells at night and now it's all cake sales and corridor-painting parties. Anyway, here's the important thing – I heard someone just then, she wouldn't repeat it to me when I asked her to, but I'm sure I heard her say she saw Mia playing with some other kid shortly before she went missing, I'm sure I heard her say 'that little scumbag'.

Edward gave him an impressed little Ooft noise and said, For the love of God don't let anyone near it. Find out who they are and claim squatter's rights if you have to, just don't let any other fucker near this.

*

When he returned to Skyler Square Ruth was smoking and crying on a porch and he put his arm around her and asked if anything had happened, and she said no not yet. I'm just sick thinking of a little kid like that all alone at night-time, it's my worst fear even now. She must be beside herself.

She recovered a little and sniffled unattractively into the sleeve of her jacket, smearing away make-up as she did so.

Oh, he would so love to go home, he would love to be anywhere, he could be in the flat taking a bath or in town having a glass of wine, he could be talking to a woman who had herself together.

He dreaded the banal misery he was sure he was about to encounter but he'd started something now and he would go on with it.

Come on, he said gently, let's get you upstairs and you can talk to me about it.

Did you get through? she asked.

Yes I told my uncle all about it, he reassured her.

4.

Once Ruth was asleep in her predictably morose quarters, Tom slipped her key into his pocket and went down into the courtyard. It was after midnight now and many of the people who'd gone out to search had arrived back. It was still warm and a few groups were outside chatting, some drinking, he was glad to see. A few of the longer-term residents on the ground floor had decided to make the most of their location and set up permanent garden furniture dining sets and sofas where the upper balconies sheltered them. If he could manage to slip into one of the chats they were facilitating he might get something good.

He was alright at this sort of thing. Despite what Edward seemed to think of him he wasn't particularly posh. His parents were standard lower-middle-class aspirational Tories. They went on a holiday to France every other year and he didn't get the jackets he asked for but nor did any of his friends so it never mattered hugely. Maybe he looked a bit posh, now, since being in London. His mother had given him a present of some money when he was moving away to buy two suits and four shirts, which had done him fine except that one of the suits he had chosen was a dark mossy green wool and on a *Sunday Mirror* placement someone asked if he was the Green Party candidate for Holborn.

He had the sort of usefully bland, agreeable, rosy face which could disappear into whatever context he wished it to. He was blond but not provocatively so. The naturally dull Kent accent could be clipped and made horsey if he was trying to get to a society party, and his father's East End adopted with relative ease when he wanted to be taken as working class.

He was wary of groups made up of only men. Sometimes their talent for automatic strata sorting was too acute and they could read something in him. It wouldn't necessarily be the truth, what they could see, but the detection of effort. With a woman or two in the mix he usually felt able to ingratiate successfully enough that a stray hint of suspicion could be overridden.

Now, he sized up the square, and settled on a group made up of two young women, one middle-aged woman, and a single older man. Manageable. They were sitting around one of the dining sets, speaking in low, nervous voices, outside number 17 which had flower baskets at its front door. They were drinking cans of beer and smoking, except for one of the younger women, a kind-looking girl in a Morrison's uniform, so he approached her first and offered a cigarette. She thanked him, smiling shyly, and he returned it for the briefest of moments before reverting to his expression of pinched worry.

I couldn't get off to sleep, knowing she's out there. It's my worst fear being alone in the dark like that, he parroted.

What's your name, you don't live in Skyler do you? asked the man, taking off his glasses to have a better look.

No, I'm a friend of Ruth's upstairs, he said nodding in the direction of the fourth floor, I moved away for a bit and I'm back looking for a flat so Ruth and her mum are letting me stay.

The table nodded with immediate, disinterested acceptance.

This was something he would never get used to; how, so often, people believed what you told them for no other reason than the fact you had said it. It seemed preposterous that they did not instantly assume any stranger asking an idle question was after something from them. There were so few moments in his life when he was not thinking about the newspaper that their happy ignorance was inconceivable. It made him feel patronisingly fond of civilians, that they had so little nous, that they would conspire in their own destruction. Sometimes they'd even invite you in after you'd actually admitted who you were. They made you a cup of tea, believing you were just thirsty after chasing around all day long, that honestly and truly you weren't like the other scummy lot out there on the porch.

He sat down without asking, but with an exhausted sigh to explain his intrusion. He sank his head into his arms for a moment as though the weight of his concern wouldn't allow him to remain standing any longer. Then he looked up.

Were any of you around when she was last playing then? What's anybody seen? It makes no sense she's just vanished into thin air.

The other young woman, not the smiling shop girl he had given the cigarette, looked at him brassily, not indulging his simpering but giving him what he wanted nonetheless, the words rushing out of her.

We all saw who she was with last. The only question is which one of them did something to that little girl.

A hot knot of excitement throbbed in his throat.

There was nothing better than this, the feeling of stepping onto the precipice of what was definitely worthwhile when you still didn't quite know what it was. He had some version of this feeling every time he broke anything, no matter how banal, he was new enough for that, but he had never stepped on anything of this order before.

Which one of them? she had said.

One of them.

Did this mean there was not just one little scumbag to root out, but perhaps – incredible, unthinkable joy – a whole lot of them?

*

TAPE RECORDING MADE BY TOM HARGREAVES, 00.35 hours

A: There are four of them up there, there used to be five.

B: The mother died about two years ago. The older mother, you know what I mean *(laughs nervously)*. Carmel's own mother, but she was the real mum in that place. She took care of them all.

A: The lot of them never seemed . . . how should I say it . . . they never seemed to be in the whole of their health. They looked tired all the time. But at least when Rose was alive the child looked well-kept.

B: They all came over at once, that was the strange thing. I know lots of Irish people, it isn't to do with that, it was just odd, the timing. They didn't come for a job, I remember Rose looking for work for ages before she found something, and her husband doesn't seem to have worked a day in his life. Carmel was seventeen already and the son, the alkie—

15

A: Richard.

B: That's right, Richard, he was an adult. Why would he move country with his parents and sister when he was grown up? It was just strange, we all found it strange. Turning up as this full family out of nowhere, not really speaking to any of the rest of us at first.

A: It made more sense when Lucy was born. Lucy is Carmel's daughter, the kid. We thought then they might have moved to London because they were too ashamed to have Carmel pregnant back home. It's not like over here, is it? It would have meant something different in Ireland. I know, my dad is Irish. I know what it's like.

B: Lucy was . . . a pretty baby.

A: No, come on, don't rewrite history (*laughing*).

B: No, I mean it! I'm serious, you just don't remember because the way she screamed, we all wanted to kill her after a while (*laughing nervously, realising what she has said*). I'm sorry, I don't mean to joke. But it's true, Lucy was a very pretty little baby with lovely big eyes, an unusual colour, almost yellow, this very, very dark hair and lashes—

A: We said they looked like they might have had some gypsy blood didn't we?

B: That's right. She was, honestly, very pretty. It was just after, the noises she would make were like nothing I'd ever heard before, and we're right below them, we got the worst of it. I didn't sleep for a year.

A: It was unholy.

B: It was beyond. It never stopped.

A: Obviously you don't blame a child for that, that's not what I'm saying, but it made them separate from everyone else because we couldn't help getting annoyed about it.

What worried me was you would hear the screaming going on and on, and then you'd see Carmel just sat out on the balcony staring into space. You couldn't even say she was ignoring it. She didn't seem to hear.

B: There was something wrong with her. And with Lucy. That seemed clear.

*

Abbreviated GP Report for ICPC (Initial Child Protection Conference), 1980

Lucy Green, aged three months, attended XXXXX Walk-in Centre at 17.20 hours on 14 March 1980. She was attended to by Dr Carole Badham. Lucy Green was accompanied by her mother, Carmel Green aged seventeen years, and grandmother Rose Green aged forty-six years. Lucy's history as stated in the notes of that date was that she was suffering from aggressive dermatitis which was causing increasing distress. The affected area had patches of broken skin. It was noted that in addition to this complaint, she was slightly underweight and suffering from an ear infection.

At 17.34 hours it was noted by Dr Badham that Carmel Green appeared listless and severely underweight. She appeared unable to engage with questions about her daughter's health history and well-being, and unable or unwilling to actively accept or note advice about how to better care for Lucy. At this point Dr Badham remained with Lucy and Carmel Green while Nurse Deirdre Whitehall took Rose into a second examination room to speak with her privately.

At 18.12 hours Nurse Whitehall noted that Rose Green was in good health and of sound mind and was realistic about the insufficiencies of her daughter's care of her granddaughter. She furthermore appeared knowledgeable about how to provide care for Lucy and about the care of babies generally. She acknowledged that the current situation was inadequate and explained that she had not immediately been available to provide more active help when Lucy was a newborn. She assured Nurse Whitehall that she was now in a position to do so.

At 18.23 hours Dr Badham spoke to Carmel and Rose Green together and prescribed an antibiotic for Lucy Green's ear infection and a fungal treatment and barrier ointment for her dermatitis. It was impressed upon both women that Dr Badham expected to see the three again in five days to check on the welfare of the baby and, should no progress be made, to discuss what the next steps must be.

On 19 March at 11.15 a.m. Lucy, Carmel and Rose Green attended the clinic again. Lucy's health appeared much improved, with dermatitis largely healed and ear infection cleared. It was agreed that with Rose now providing primary care for Lucy, no further action was necessary but that regular check-ups would continue.

*

TAPE RECORDING MADE BY TOM HARGREAVES, 01.27 hours

A: At first we didn't see much of any of them, except Richard when he was pissed, when he went out for fags or coming back from the pub. But when Lucy was a few months old, Rose took charge of things. She took the baby out for walks in her pram and painted their front door, she seemed to be shaping it up inside as well from what I could see. She never invited me in, but she was lovely actually. Very kind, warm sort of a person. We never got into any big conversations – I didn't ever ask outright why they had moved over here or what life had been like back home, but she always remembered what my two were up to and asked after them, and we'd talk about what was going on around the estate. Carmel did go with her on the walks but for a long time she said barely anything. She just stood alongside while Rose chatted and showed off the baby. Don't get me wrong, there was nobody pretending Lucy belonged to Rose. We had all seen Carmel in her last month of pregnancy – God! It was awful, a girl so slight as that, it didn't look right – but the impression I got was, Rose had taken over the mothering for the time being. And things seemed alright for them, for a while.

It's late, I'm going in now. Shouldn't you head back up to Ruth?

5.

The office of the *Daily Herald* was in Southwark and each morning Tom walked across the bridge from his flat in Whitechapel, he felt a moment of golden pleasure to be doing so. He glanced with derision at tourists taking photos on this bridge which he used every day, used for function. It was his bridge as much as it could be any man's and he tried to remember how lucky that made him. He tried to remember to turn and absorb the city on either side, even when it was barely visible in drizzle.

Some of his friends had gone to Australia or Asia after they'd left university, but who would struggle to love the sight of a beach or a forest? What sort of achievement would it be to gain mastery over a small portion of picturesque nature? Plenty of others had moved to London but may as well have been in any other English suburb, so minimal were their interactions with the place they lived. They got mortgages and girlfriends and spoke about their houses as though houses were worlds. But Tom actually lived in

London, he worked scraping beneath the stones, learning its people, he moved around it fluently and swiftly, and in the mornings he allowed himself the brief thrill of self-congratulation for having chosen this hardship.

It was Thursday morning and Mia was dead.

He had filed the piece reporting a family statement delivered by her uncle. The uncle – a diffident bespectacled man in a hideous jumper Tom predicted he would come to regret wearing – had stood outside the Enright home. The flat had all of its curtains drawn, and as he spoke he held up two photographs of Mia beseechingly to the reporters who had gathered. There weren't many. The turnaround between her going missing and her body being found was only sixteen hours, and unlike Tom the others had not been there in the interim to absorb the tension of foul play. To them it may still have been a tragic accident, a little girl fallen down or hit by a car, something newsworthy but ultimately forgettable.

As far as he was aware it was only he who had pressed hard enough to get the information about bruising to her neck, and he knew for sure it was only he who had been in the square last night to hear the half-pissed speculation from neighbours that Mia was last seen playing with a kid known universally as trouble, one from a rotten family, one who may have been capable of harming a toddler. Now that she was dead they might think twice before carelessly spewing speculation about, so it was a bit of luck he had caught them beforehand. But he knew there was almost no time before every other journalist gathered as much as he already had, and he needed to agree a strategy for what was next.

*

The first day he met Edward, eight months before Mia Enright went missing, he knew he was about to begin an inevitable course of romantic, somewhat filial longing. He

20

knew, too, from experience that these crushes came and went and that he would eventually satisfy or surprise Edward, or be let down by him, in a way which meant the yearning was no longer acute, did not hold daily sway in his life. There had been the beautiful priest at school with whom he discussed Shakespeare and whose wide anguished mouth had haunted his thoughts for a year. Father Rowan had been left behind once it became clear that Tom would only win a place in his heart by committing to purity and temperance with his own totality. Even to a dreamy and pious fourteen-year-old this was an impossible prospect.

Later in sixth form there was a boy of his own age but built like an oak tree and with a full beard and an apparently comprehensive knowledge of the works of Walter Benjamin and Adorno. He was also named Tom and to Tom Hargreaves' delight their peers would sometimes refer to them as The Toms when they burrowed together studying or furiously smoking.

That romance had ended when the larger of the Toms one day tried to materialise it, inclining his dense beard which was laden with the smoke of his absurd pipe. Tom had been conciliatory and polite in his refusal, but it had confirmed that his crushes were made meaningful to him only through their continued latency. There were a few others in university, charismatic lecturers and mature students, but he had never wished to please anyone as he wished to please Edward.

They shared a quality, which was to be very clever but not about anything in particular. They were imbued with talent and had always felt this in themselves, but had struggled to find clear uses for the mysterious skills which they felt simmering. Many people suffered from feelings of thwarted greatness and endured them with only moderate regret, but Tom and Edward were alike because they were determined to be the best, to succeed despite the knowledge they were not quite excellent at anything. Edward had shown Tom that this was possible, that newspapers were a place to do it. All you had to remember was to never, ever stop.

Do you know the difference between me and most people who want my job, Tom? Edward had asked him in the pub after his first day, And, I hope, the difference between you and the other kids who wanted your new job? It's that they give themselves a break. I don't mean every now and then, or when their dad dies or they get meningitis, I mean they give themselves a break almost always. They want to finish in time for a nice dinner, and they want to see plenty of the ill sister or the kids or the girlfriend. All you have to do to get to where I am and beyond is to stick around longer and want it more than those people, and to not want what they want. You can't want to stop.

It was easy to see this was true of Edward. He was, in his mid-forties, slender and ropily muscled, like a tired but still vicious old big cat in a zoo. He was handsome in an incidental way, a way you would never assume he noticed himself and which was undermined by the hollows beneath the cheekbones and above his eyes. He was dishevelled, but appealingly so, greying hair always unwashed and overlong but the effect of disarray easily softened by a rotation of incredibly expensive overcoats and decent suits kept dry-cleaned and hanging in his office for when he needed to rush to a dinner with advertisers or a politician's aide. He appeared to have a lot of sex but also to regard it with the same neutral disinterest as he did everything outside the newspaper, and this in particular was attractive to Tom. The idea of women being functional instead of frustratingly beguiling, of them being easily acquired and just as easily lost rather than taking up unhappy residence in his head for months at a time. That was power. That was freedom.

*

He arrived at the great ugly glistening building which he loved so much.

On one of his first mornings a memo had been sent around from Edward to the desks of the entire editorial staff, which read:

A REMINDER! Reasonable excuses for lateness/ missing meetings/not doing something I told you to do etc, include: Bereavement (parent only). Serious illness (life-threatening, your own). Reasonable excuses do NOT INCLUDE ordinary human failings such as hangovers, broken hearts, etc etc etc.

In the early weeks, he was forced to spend precious minutes laboriously spelling and respelling his name while the security manager rang upstairs to check he was supposed to be there, making him late and flustered when he could least afford to be. He was surprised by the excessive scrutiny, until an old-timer had explained the office had received bomb threats during the Wapping strike and the building's owners had been paranoid ever since.

It wasn't threats from the inkies themselves, it was from some communists, student types – did look a bit like you I imagine, actually, so maybe that's why you're getting stopped, he said and twitched his large moustache with purposeful amusement.

Since the issues had ceased and he gained access each morning with sublime, swift ease, he enjoyed these moments as much as any in his day. He relished the manly nod exchanged with the guards sitting at the front desk, the implied approval of their disinterest. It was a clean, good part of life. It assured him of the ongoingness of things, regardless of how disastrously the previous day had concluded, or how badly he feared the one about to begin. In the lift his bowels creaked with anxious excitement.

He allowed himself to think through what it would be like if he shit himself here in the lift. What would actually happen? He would have to feign an extravagant mental breakdown, he supposed. He could work himself up into a fit while he waited for someone to come. He would never be able to return to work then, but at least he would have the grace and dignity of the fully mad. Since childhood he had forced himself to calculate what the worst and most inappropriate action he could take at any given time would be. Going to see the Christmas pantomime with his mother had become a yearly torture as he sat writhing in his seat, helplessly picturing himself leaping from his seat and onto the stage, where he would remove all of his clothes in a violent flourish.

In Edward's office he explained the situation as it currently stood. Firstly, what had been a functional but ultimately forgettable tear-jerker – a cute little kid coming to harm – seemed on its way to becoming a murder case. Secondly, it appeared that legitimate suspicion was being directed toward another child – and not just a child but a girl. Thirdly, this girl belonged to a family of misanthropic Irish degenerates who, it was fair to assume, lived at least partially off the welfare state and had offered nothing but parasitic consumption (and now a horrific crime) to the great nation of Britain they had seen fit to settle in.

Edward listened carefully and then asked, What about the other family, the little girl's? What do they feel like?

Tom told him. They were in many ways the benevolent inverse of the Green family. Mum and Dad were Charles and Etta, Etta a shift worker in a care home and Charles a sort of community jack of all trades, helping to run homework and art clubs for local kids funded by the council. In his spare time he led an amateur dramatics group for adults.

Their son Elliott was twelve and well liked in school and on the estate, helping his dad out with the clubs when needed, polite and good-looking and not overly friendly with any of the more, shall we say, earthy young lads on the estate.

There was a silence as Edward thought.

It could be interesting, could it not? he asked. Say this is true, to whatever degree, say the kid of Family Bad Apples has maybe killed the kid of Family Do-Gooder. Even if it doesn't bear out in the end, or doesn't come to trial, or get a conviction, it could be interesting in the meantime. Nineties Britain, the Battle of the Council Estate; feckless foreign wanderers with a whiff of abuse and chaos turn on the Deserving Poor.

Tom felt gratified by the seriousness with which Edward was taking his story, seeing it as a major, state-of-the-nation type piece. There was a formerly fringe politician named Jim Godfrey – a brash, blokey fellow in loud jackets and with shovel-like hands, often seen grasping a pint and a fag – who had lately been making some dramatic leaps. The *Daily Herald* was interested in his project because he was once a senior trade unionist who had quit his position in disgust, claiming the honourable tradition set by his father was now ruined, infiltrated by communists and grifters. One of his big political gambits was divvying up the poor, just as Edward had – the feral doomed kind, migrants and sexual degenerates and the idle, as opposed to the traditional, decent poor.

Okay, here's what we'll do, said Edward, use what connections you've got already to go and stay very close to the Bad Apples. Don't bother trying to get the dead kid's family on side, we'll send someone else to try and get something from them. If they're as you say they are, there's not a lot to get excited about there anyway.

You need to stick with the other family. If there's questioning or an arrest, we're going to get them a safe house, because their neighbours are going to be out with pitchforks pretty soon. And if it all goes off well, we'll have them in a hotel where only we have access to them by the time anyone else gets wind of this. We'll give them a few quid and as much booze as they can drink, and you'll go in too and see what comes out of their mouths once they trust you. And I want you talking to the kid's school, anyone who knew her, anyone who can say they saw her doing something sad, bad or mad, yes?

Yes, Tom thought. Yes, this is what I have waited for.

*

The next morning, after the police released further details, Edward sat down in his office and wrote.

Friday 18 May 1990
EDITORIAL
WHO KILLED BABY MIA? SOUTH
LONDON COMMUNITY IN SHOCK
AS FOUL PLAY CONFIRMED

All parents share a terror which we can barely acknowledge until we are forced to. It's the stuff of nightmares, twisted fairy tales, and urban legends – until it becomes reality. One inconsolable London couple were last night grappling with evil infiltrating their neighbourhood and their family. Charles and Etta Enright are being looked after by heartbroken family and friends in the aftermath of their precious three-year-old daughter's death. Etta is reportedly unable to eat, sleep, or even stand unassisted. This mother without a child has gone into a perfectly understandable state of shock. Who knows if she will ever emerge, and what sort of life awaits her if she does? Charles, a community leader, is trying to remain strong to support their older child Elliott – a popular athletic student at local St Barnaby's School, neighbours told the *Herald*. But there is only so much a father can withstand, and Charles is as devastated as his wife.

To lose a child is always lifelong agony for parents who had expected to grow old with their beloved daughters and sons.

But there are some tragedies which can be withstood, and others which can't.

If Mia had slipped away after an illness, or even hit by a speeding car, there would be some logic to her loss. The world is cruel, and terrible accidents and mysteries happen. We all have to accept a certain level of misfortune in our lives. As things stand, her death is a senseless act of brutality which would have been avoided if not for the wicked urges of a monster. We now know that Mia, who weighed two stone and four pounds, who loved her mother brushing her curly blonde hair, whose favourite food was jam and porridge, was suffocated and left like a bag of rubbish down an alley next to the bins.

Somebody chose to to terrify her and then take her life away like it meant nothing. But it did mean something. It meant everything. The family of this beloved little girl, her neighbours, the people of London, and the people of Britain – all of us deserve to feel safe and to know that the subhuman creature who did this can't hurt any more children, will be swiftly apprehended and will pay dearly for what they have done.

He felt a whisper of gooseflesh on his neck as he finished that one, tears stinging in his eyes.

6.
St Barnaby's School

Miss Serena Dillon was easy to speak to for several reasons. She was a lovely woman, an alluring mix of wholesome benevolence and sexy authority, as all twentysomething primary schoolteachers ought to be. She favoured esoteric androgynous clothes which looked stylish on the foreign but insane on the English. Most importantly she wanted to be a writer, which made her want to interest and flatter Tom.

Although he doubted her childhood dreams had involved doorstepping grieving parents and dreaming up splashes about heroin-addicted traffic wardens, nevertheless he was technically paid to write and this made him someone to impress. He noticed how her face opened up when she learned what he did. She became not just pretty but beautiful, her guard splintered in an instant, and he let her tell him about herself and her ambitions before he began poking about for gossip about Lucy and the other Greens. Her skin was sallow and her nose sharp and he wondered with idle arousal if she might be Greek (a post-school lads' holiday to Crete had left him with an enduring imprint of sexual awe for Greek women, all the irritable daughters of the bar owners rolling their eyes at the drunk English).

When he had heard about her teenage poetry prize and her student journalism and her novel stashed in a drawer at home and her new dream of writing a children's book he lost patience and made a clumsy, regrettable segue.

A children's book, how nice, and is this the sort of book a child like Lucy might enjoy?

Miss Dillon's eyes narrowed and she disliked him then at once for his lack of finesse, but decided to speak anyway.

Why, he wondered, why do they speak?

He sensed no malice in this woman, no need to gossip. It was, he thought, perhaps that Lucy had been troubling her for some time and nobody had listened. Or more terribly for her, now that Lucy was implicated in a crime, it was possible she had never brought herself to say anything aloud at all. It was possible, he reflected, that she would regret it for the rest of her life, and she had not yet realised this.

These were the people who kept him from sleeping, when anybody did. Not the victims themselves, whose absences he felt to be dreadful but endurable in their inevitability. He had never known them in life, they appeared to him only as the dead people they would now always be. Nor was it even necessarily those who loved the dead people most – who were ruined and drained by their grief, who screamed at God – who struck him.

It was usually those like Miss Dillon who harboured private suspicions but who did not act boldly, did not voice their suspicions, and who would come to learn that, if they had, they could have spared somebody's suffering, or even their whole life.

One case he had seen written up in his first month at the *Herald* had to do with the accidental death of a neglected five-year-old, whose mother had carried on a campaign of abuse sporadic enough to evade notice. The child's paternal grandmother suspected at one point, months before the eventual death, that something was not right and contacted social services, but was rebuffed. Then again three weeks before the death. Again, nothing happened. Suddenly for whatever hellish reason the pitch and frequency of the mistreatment escalated and the child died soon after.

Tom thought of the grandmother often, twisting inside her mind and imagining how it would feel to have been the one to correctly identify how wrong things were, and yet not to have stopped the worst from happening. You would, surely, never think of anything again except that you ought to have gone in and taken the child, stolen the child, bulldozed down the front door if that was what it took.

This was my first year with Lucy but I had heard a few things before I taught her, Miss Dillon said. This was before her grandmother died – Rose I think she was called. Her behaviour was better before I got her, before the grandmother's death, but bad enough I'd got wind of it.

Then there had been a game, while she was on playground duty one morning last year. It was almost too embarrassing for her to say it but it was called 'IRA'. Yes, she knew how that sounded, she wasn't trying to suggest anything genuinely untoward, but Lucy had introduced this game called IRA to her classmates. She said when they were caught that her cousins in Ireland had played it with her, though when they asked the mother about it she had told the school that Lucy had never met any cousins, had never been back to Ireland, it was just a fantasy, something she had picked up from other Irish kids or her uncle reminiscing.

There had been a version of the same game years before in the school, called Bash Code or something like that. There was a suggestion that these cousins who had taught it to her back home on her holidays – the ones who had never existed – really were IRA adjacent, and frankly Lucy did nothing to minimise that suggestion. That's the way children are. Sometimes they want to fit in but sometimes they long for a mark of notoriety, something to be recalled by. The school had made an announcement and forbidden it, but it looked just like any other chase game from a distance so it was difficult to police.

In the game there was a code word. The children on one side had different letters which made it up, and the other team had to get the letters out of them to break the code. They beat each other up to get them.

And Lucy hurt somebody during one of these games? Tom asked her.

He watched her recede further into retrospective concern as she had spoken and became swept up in it himself, burrowing into the crease between her eyes, sharing the plaintive dismay she had conjured by thinking about a child giving substantial pain to another child. That kind of transaction held no meaning, suffering without reason. It was distasteful to think about, even this minor precursor to what had eventually come.

Yes, Lucy hurt a boy, she said, nothing lasting but he needed stitches. She had him on the ground and she hit his cheek with a stone twice and cut him. She's tiny, you know? I'm not sure if you've seen that. So it was a bizarre scene. He's a nice boy, gentle, I think he wasn't putting up any resistance because she's a girl and a foot shorter than he is. It took me far too long to register what was happening, how bad it was. They had all been laughing a minute before.

It was Lucy's screaming which alerted Miss Dillon, although she didn't tell this to Tom.

The boy, Gregory, was weeping also but not hysterical. Lucy was howling at an ungodly pitch, her hand pressed against the wound on his face, bloody stone cast aside. Her hands were dirty with it and with leaves and grit from the ground and Miss Dillon thought in the mental looseness of her shock that she was packing it in, putting dirt inside him.

She lifted Lucy easily away, marvelling at her remarkable lightness, the jagged little legs thrashing uselessly. She lost track of her in the immediate aftermath, taking Gregory inside and strapping a makeshift bandage to his cheek and calling his mother.

After that, when he was sniffling bravely and being looked after by the kindly school secretary, she went to the boys' toilets. They were the ancient ones which hadn't been refurbished so were generally not populated, a place she

31

could come to be alone when she needed to, to put on make-up before a date or breathe heavily through a frustrated urge toward unkindness. When she opened the door Lucy was standing there, so small that her head was almost level with a sink, which she was striking her forehead against, with silent, eerily efficient brutality.

Lucy, said Miss Dillon weakly, stop, stop, please, stop.

And she did, looking up in a moment of indecision, those curious yellow eyes, before running past Miss Dillon and away around the corridor corner before it was really clear what should happen, how to reasonably respond.

The thing she had witnessed had seemed to her so ugly, something rent from a terrible unknowable privacy, that it defied description or standard professional reportage.

When she got home that evening she was still pretending to herself that she would inform somebody the following morning. She recalled later in the night that it was Friday and there would be no school for three days because of a bank holiday and then she knew she would never tell anybody what she had seen.

The image cracked and disseminated with every minute, becoming harder to summarise and harder to defend letting slip away without intervention.

Lucy's act was becoming smaller and bigger than it had been in its actual occurrence – she was just messing around; actually no she was going to give herself brain damage; maybe, yes, no.

She was a tiny rabid black-haired demon from hell.

No, that wasn't right, she was a sad little girl.

It was easier to decide to briefly be someone who hadn't seen it. In her own small flat with all the comforting plants and the super-sized *Vertigo* poster. She stayed in that Friday night but called her brother and some friends to make enough plans for the rest of the weekend that she would have no time to herself. Saturday would be consumed by getting ready and then lunch in town somewhere and going out in the evening. Sunday would be filled with the resulting hangover and a roast lunch with a brother she rarely bothered to see, where she would have enough red wine to fall asleep early. When she woke up it would be time to have to do things again, and these immediate obligations would free her of the now ephemeral obligation of witnessing what she had.

Why, she thought to herself that Friday night, why had she called her brother Seb to see her on Sunday? She had known he'd say yes, that was perhaps a point in his favour, but neither of them could relax together. At home for Christmas they were sometimes forced to acknowledge the unfortunate coincidence of them both having ended up in London which meant their never seeing each other was remarkable and negative. The rest of the family she could not-see as much as she pleased because of logistics, but with him it had to be apologised for, and fantasy hypothetical arrangements made to appease the onlooking relatives.

It was not that she disliked him. His life, unrecognisable as it was – working in 'energy', living in Kidbrooke, father to two fat baby boys – was unseemly to her as hers must have been to him. They had shared the unique burden of their childhood, stood guard over it together, so that now in the absence of that duty they were lost and useless before one another.

She knew, really, why she had phoned Seb, and why, too, she had allowed Lucy to run away. It was because of her older sister Eloise. In the tiny village where they had grown up, Eloise's unusual body had already been accepted and adjusted to by the time Serena was born. A small community can be judgemental and harsh, but it also has the advantage of familiarity, and Eloise after all was a sweet-natured and pretty-faced five-year-old girl. Her differences – the shortened limbs and a dramatically

33

arched spine – were not so notable in an infant, and by the time they became notable her family and neighbours already knew and loved her. Serena did not grow up feeling Eloise was someone to hide away, or who caused other people unhappiness with her presence. Eloise was her funny older sister, even when Serena swiftly outgrew her in tallness. The few times some kid had tried to bully Eloise, she had either dismissed them witheringly or Seb had intervened and beat them up.

This changed when Serena was becoming a teenager. She passed by Eloise's room one night and, glancing idly inside, saw that her back was shaking, suppressing sobs. She was appalled to feel a surge of visceral, repulsed alarm at the sight, the tininess of the body unclothed, the painful-looking angle of her spine and neck. Her sister may have been crying about any number of things, but Serena wasn't able to ask what they were. Instead she suspected that Eloise was in far worse pain than had ever been known, suffering in the recesses of a privacy so total that it was almost evil. She had never fully lost this terror of the private suffering of other people, nor the shame of wanting not to see it.

7.

The police came quietly to 168 Skyler Square at dusk on a Saturday to take Lucy Green, ten years and five months old.

Multiple neighbours had made reports to police that she was the last one seen with Mia Enright before her death, leading her away from the square where they were playing. She had a history of violence and came from a questionable family. Some added their own stories about the Greens, Lucy saying strange things to their kids, inciting dangerous games, Richard talking to himself, John's hermit status and his unnerving staring when he emerged, Carmel's wan superiority (floating disdainfully through their world as though she wasn't a part of it, as if she didn't really live among them). Lucy's ill-fitting clothes, sporadically appalling hygiene, compulsive spitting.

It was all by the wayside, what mattered was they had seen her.

They had seen her walking off with that poor child, and they wanted answers.

There was some confusion at the door when they arrived. Incorrect information had been fed to them somewhere down the line that Lucy was sixteen, so that when Carmel opened the door they mistook her momentarily for her daughter, both of them slender and spiky and dark. They were under orders to not draw attention to themselves and were speaking in low assuring tones but Carmel was ruining that with her noisy confusion which had brought neighbours out to their balconies to watch.

She looked at the police, insulted, and said loudly, I am not Lucy!

They apologised and said that they needed to speak with Lucy about the events of 16 May when Mia Enright had gone missing.

Come in then, Carmel said.

They told her it would be better if Lucy came to the station so they could speak to her properly, and that her parent or parents or guardian should come with her now, and that they would explain everything there.

I am the guardian, I am the child's mother, she said to them, in an almost apologetic tone, as though this changed something and they would have to rethink, but they didn't.

They stepped inside the door to wait as Carmel went to find Lucy and get her things. It wasn't nearly as bad as the worst places, but it was bad enough. Where Richard sat, by the television, there were cans topped with ash and food wrappers stuffed into crevices. These radiated outward from the nucleus of his body in various states of age, a visual timeline like the inner circles of a cut tree.

Carmel called for Lucy, going first into the bedroom they shared, and then into her father's room, vacant with its bed made neatly, and finally the bathroom where the child was crouching between the base of the toilet and an old footstool kept beside it laden with damp books and magazines. The narrow space between the two meant she was wedged in tightly, pressure exerted from either side, soothing.

Come on Lucy, put your coat on, we have to go out for a bit now, said her mother.

I can't, said Lucy, rigid and pale.

You don't have a choice, the police need to ask you something about Mia. It's important. It won't take long, they need to know everything that happened so they can catch the man who did it.

I can't Mummy, she moaned.

Carmel, always vaguely nauseated by that word, the simpering, foreign priss of it, grabbed Lucy by the arm and yanked her up, pulling her good coat around her shoulders. She ran the cold tap and pushed Lucy's face beneath it for a moment to calm the redness of her tear-streaked face. She dried her off with a scratchy blue hand towel and smoothed her hair down, Lucy's eyes closing in pleasure at this sensation despite it all.

The coat was a brown fake fur that her grandmother Rose had found in one of the good charity shops near a house she cleaned. It was Lucy's favourite thing over the Christmas holidays that year until she had gone back to school and a girl she had been best friends with the term before, but who had moved on to another girl now, laughed at it and called it cheap. This was what she was wearing when she left the flat and was first seen as a murderer. Neighbours mostly watched through windows or from balconies, but a few had emerged to gather near the door. Two people took photographs. One was an amateur, a neighbourhood crank, the other a freelance professional who stood a few feet back next to Tom. Tom had no idea when or if they could use a photo like this, hadn't yet got up to speed with what they could and couldn't do about kids, but he wanted pictures just in case.

He registered two things as he first got sight of the Greens. The first was that Lucy looked nothing like the feral, sinister child he had imagined. She was tiny in her big foolish fuzzy coat, face pinched and panicking. She held a policeman's hand on one side and grasped for her mother's on the other, but Carmel's arm hung listless and unmoved by her need. The second thing Tom registered was that Carmel wasn't only unusual and ghostly in her appearance, as he had been told already, but was also remarkably beautiful in her way. The ample black brows were lustrous, glossy, and set in a bold frown toward the clumps of onlookers. (Who, he noted, were stirring, one man spitting near the Greens. He was only resisting doing more because nobody else had yet, but if one struck out then they all would, things would get bad quickly.)

She had a proud high forehead and burning red cheeks. He could see what her detractors had meant about how strident she was, superior, but he looked at the steeliness of her gaze and saw something else. It was something he wanted to get inside of and break apart.

*

In the police station they gave Lucy hot chocolate after hot chocolate. It was decided that Carmel wouldn't be her guardian because she made the child too upset and was creating a disturbance. But Lucy would have a social worker called Margie and her grandad would come in if she wanted him too. They just needed some questions answered and it would all be alright.

The room smelled like paint. Lucy liked the smell, and it was like when Rose had taken them to get passports in the police station before she died.

Why does it always smell like paint? she asked the policemen.

Ah, we like to keep it freshly done, one of them said, the bigger, nicer fellow with a fantastic black moustache.

The tape was set on.

Now Lucy, we know you were out playing a few days ago, said the big moustache.

His colleague, the thin fair bald man, added: Some of your neighbours saw you playing in the square that day.

Lucy said: What day?

Bald man: You know which one. We're here about Mia going away.

Lucy: Yeah. I was playing. I was playing that night.

Moustache: What night? Were you playing with Mia that day? It was in the day you were last seen with Mia.

Lucy: We were playing, lots of us. There was a game on.

Bald man: The last anyone else saw of Mia was you taking her off. And then, Lucy, you know that we found Mia later, and she wasn't alive?

Lucy: I don't know. What do you mean? I don't know. *(panicking)*

Moustache: Where was the last place you saw Mia, Lucy?

Lucy: Playing.

Moustache: No, where was it, Lucy, the place you last saw Mia when you were playing?

Lucy: We were behind the bins. It was a game.

Moustache: I know it was. That's okay. You need to tell us about the game.

Lucy: Rose, I want Rose, Rose, Rose, Rose, Rose, I want Rose. *(panicking)*

(Brief intervention from social worker)

(Break; Lucy's grandfather John Green brought in)

38

Moustache: Okay Lucy we heard you say you didn't mean anything, but we need you to tell us what happened. Would you be able to repeat what you just told us when the tape was off do you think? Try to explain it to Grandad.

Lucy: It was a game called Freak Show.

Bald man: You should try to say what happened from start to finish.

Lucy *(calling outside the room)*: Oh Jesus, Mummy believe me. Please let Mummy believe me.

(Break)

Lucy *(sobbing)*: The game was that you do something unusual or mad, that was all. It was only part of the game. You held your breath until you went blue. And I was bringing Mia into the game. *(Looking at her guardian and her grandfather)* God you don't believe me. You don't believe me. Grandad you have to believe me. Ah, no. Ah, no. I didn't. I didn't. I didn't. *(sobbing)*

I never did.

Please, God, I never did.

I never did, no, no, no.

Part II

1.
Hotel Gargano, Saturday 19 May

It was near eleven by the time the car dropped them off. Carmel looked at the remnants of light through the car window. They mocked her, God refusing to let this worst day end.

With the thought came a brief, surprised calibration – this was the worst day now, and that was new. The former worst day had seemed permanent and irrevocable, but it wasn't. It had been replaced, and maybe she would never even think of it again. It occurred to her, not for the first time in her life, that the only surefire way to reduce a problem's importance was to replace it with a new and more urgent problem. Maybe that was the solution, she thought. Maybe she need only get new, more pressing problems all the time, to reduce the importance of their precedents. She could run out now and kill somebody herself, for instance, grab a baby from a pram and dash it on the pavement. Then she would only have to worry about that for the time being, not about what Lucy had done, and when that problem stopped being as urgent, she could cut off her arm, or contract a fatal disease, or even get pregnant again.

The helpful policeman who accepted regular envelopes from Tom and other *Daily Herald* reporters had dropped them off at Hotel Gargano, near Mornington Crescent. It was at the end of a row of houses, isolated by its overgrown hedges and substantial gated courtyard. Hotel Gargano was once almost elegant and was now almost quaint. Its elderly proprietor Leonard was the father-in-law of Robert Eccles on the Entertainment desk. Robert made sure that when sources needed sequestering Leonard got the business, the newspaper paying three times the going rate to book the place out and guarantee privacy. This constituted an excess of caution. Hotel Gargano had only six bedrooms, and rarely were any occupied except by those beleaguered foot-baller mistresses, and government ministers contemplating photos of themselves between boys' legs in public toilets.

In between their stays, very occasional tourists would happen across the hotel and be hosted with sighing reluc-tance by Leonard, who did not need the money and kept his establishment nominally open so that he had a place to maintain a well-stocked bar. He allowed his son-in-law's paper to put up their anxious miscreants not for the fees but from curiosity and the sporadic excitement of a fallen woman drinking morosely with him into the wee hours. Because he was not mean and had no shortage of money, and because he spent much of his own time there, the build-ing was not damp or cold. It was only odd and a little haunted, furnishings and blankets in some of the unused rooms clean but unchanged for decades, the smell of inertia rising drily when they were disturbed.

Richie regarded it from the porch, waiting for his father to laboriously exit the car. When they had mentioned being put up in a hotel he had imagined a modern kind with the big anonymous rounded bars which stayed open until guests stopped drinking. This looked to be the abandoned home of a rich madman; he worried there would be no minibar in the rooms, and he could not go out to get any-thing. The policeman had impressed upon them before their departure the importance of staying put once they had been deposited here. He had looked at Richard with disgust and spoken loudly and slowly as one would to a thick kid.

You may not understand the sort of situation you and your family are in, Mr Green, he said. There are people out there tonight who would pay good money for the privilege of hurting any or all of your family. It is imperative you do not set foot out of the premises until we know how Lucy's situation is progressing. Okay?

Richard nodded back to say that it was okay, but the policeman took his silence as a further provocation.

You weren't in the room, so you might not know as well as your sister and your father do. Lucy looks to have done something very, very serious indeed. Some people would call it evil. And from what I can tell you don't have a lot of defenders waiting for you back at your flat. Away from there and hidden is the only safe place for you.

Richie was not stupid. He was not deluded enough to think that his mind was operating at the same level it had been fifteen years ago, before its daily batterings, but he had not lost his basic grip on things. The glaze which some mistook for pure idiocy or self-inflicted brain damage was intentional, and when it had not been recently enough stoked with a drink, he disappeared into himself until one could be found. As the policeman spoke, Richie was not incapable of taking in the information, but he did feel a great resistance, wrenching behind his eyes back toward the base of his skull, trying to reach toward the last remaining traces of the final drink he had taken before this nightmare began.

The policeman was correct that Richie's absence from the questioning room (though he could hear its awful noises dimly from where he sat in the corridor) had made what was unfolding feel false and almost laughable. He hadn't learned about the toddler going missing, or being found dead, until after everyone else on the square. Or maybe he had known, maybe he had been told several times over, and forgotten each one. He would never know because he didn't remember any of that day clearly. Not before they'd come in the door hunting Lucy, opening his door and exposing him to all the gawking neighbours trying to get a good look. His throat closed with indignation at the memory of it, his chair and his rubbish and his drinks laid bare. Not that he cared, really, what they thought of him. It was more the conjured presence of Rose, the idea of her mortification. Thank God – thank God! – she wasn't here to see this, he thought.

To see him, and his ever decreasing world, revealed in an ugly instant to people outside the family. To see Carmel worse than before she died. It would have been hard for her to imagine that there was a figure more upsetting than the wan, useless ghost Carmel was when they moved to London, but since Rose died she had become worse than useless and was instead active, fizzing, alive with her sourness. That was when she could be bothered to behave any sort of way toward anyone in the family. Half the time she was out and wouldn't say where, and the rest she spent lying in the bedroom like it was a tomb, ignoring the daughter she shared it with.

Lucy.

How would Rose have coped with seeing Lucy now? To hear her anguished howls from the interview room, and to know, to suspect, that she might have hurt another child? He could not bring himself, even in the privacy of his own mind, to think of the word 'kill', much less 'murder'. The thought would stick there on the word 'hurt' and never be able to move fully to the other, truer words. He knew it was the one thing to be thankful for now that Rose wasn't around to see the circus, to see what had become of the family she had given up her own life to try and hold together. It would put her in the grave all over again. He needed a drink.

John made his way finally to the entrance, having taken his time getting needlessly helped out of the car by the police officer.

Why, thought Richie, as he watched the show of weakness. Could it be he was enjoying the attention?

The three Greens stood outside the door, a grand old bright red one, waiting to be told what to do. There was a pretty hand-painted sign to its right, emerging from overrun greenery. It said Hotel Gargano in intricate lettering beside a picture of green grapes.

Here we are for our family holiday at last, Mam, thought Carmel.

Just ring the buzzer and go on inside, he knows you're coming, said the policeman.

What about the money and all? asked Carmel.

It will be sorted out for you, he'll tell you what to do, and he was off then.

Leonard opened the door for them. Welcome, welcome, he said, ushering them in.

We don't even have our stuff, Carmel said, realising.

That's alright, Miss, there are robes and towels in the rooms, Leonard said.

No, she said, flustered, I mean we don't have anything at all. We didn't get to go home first. I haven't so much as a change of underwear, and neither do they, gesturing with anger at her father and brother.

I think you'll find yourself looked after soon, if you'd like to go through to the bar there's someone waiting for you to discuss what happens next.

Richard's brain felt cool instantly, the bar and the idea of a person who would tell them what to do.

The bar was a comfortable back room, red upholstery and wood everywhere which made Richard think fondly of pubs at home. He could have cried with relief at the smell of whisky and spilt beer on carpet. He must find some cigarettes and then everything would be alright.

A man was sitting at the counter, wearing a nice wool jacket and thoughtfully regarding them over the pint he was nursing. Carmel recognised him at once as the handsome one from outside the flat. She'd noticed because he didn't look like he lived there, she'd never seen him before. He met her eye and nodded at her, and then at her father who was trailing uncertainly in the door way, and at Richie, to whom he indicated the empty stool beside him.

Hello, he said, I'm Tom. I'm here to help you.

2.

In the end it was much easier than Tom had anticipated.

He had come prepared with all sorts of pretty speeches and logical arguments and even some veiled threats if it got really difficult.

He had forgotten how easy it is to offer something to people who had nothing.

They had no particular prejudices against his paper, seemed not to read papers of any sort. When he gently suggested that they might be expected to have some conversations with him – just natural and informal talks which would give him an idea of what they were like as a family, what Lucy was like, try to get any misconceptions straightened – they did not appear put out or concerned. Rather, Carmel and Richard didn't, and their father sat in poised silence, letting Tom talk on.

He was an odd-looking man, Tom thought. Some parts were gone to rot as he had expected from the neighbours' descriptions, like the unkempt beard turned yellow for inches around the mouth, and the distended belly from ill nutrition and beer. But he had strikingly blue, lively eyes, and the features of his broad watchful face were strangely youthful, the nose still a bit upturned like a cartoon schoolboy's, cheeks round and unlined.

I'll be surprised if I get much from him, thought Tom.

But that wouldn't matter if he didn't interfere with his off-spring talking freely.

So that's it, more or less, that's the deal, he finished. You'll stay here in the hotel for a few days, maybe a week. From my side of the bargain that means you can't talk to any other newspapers, can't talk to anyone at all in fact, you just stay here. From your side it means you're safe from prying eyes, no need to worry about anything in this time of great stress. If and when you need to go in and out to visit Lucy, you'll have a driver. Each of you will be paid a hundred pounds per day that you stay here. We'll cover whatever hotel expenses you run up.

The old man seemed somewhat placated by this final offering, and Tom wondered if it would be a sort of end-of-the-world extravagance for him.

Tom had covered a story in his first month of work experience back in Kent, some local hippies who thought their tarot cards or whatever rubbish it was had shown the world was going to end on 13 April 1983. It hadn't, but they had partied so much, leaving the beach in catastrophic ruins, that their hangovers must have felt like it had.

John Green had the countenance of a man who had not been treated to many things, who knew that there was nothing given freely in this world – but maybe it was the case that his life had been rendered so nonsensical and dreadful that he was willing to accept the poisoned chalice now, and drink all he could from it before the world went entirely dry and dark.

Will there be a cap on the expenses? Richard asked, calm in the face of Carmel's furious embarrassment. It was a fair question, after all.

There's no cap, Tom said with a thin smile, In fact I think you should see this as a totally limitless situation, when it comes to that. Food and drink. I think under the circumstances you could all do with cutting loose a bit, don't you?

I do, said Richard, as it happens I do indeed.

*

They sat in the bar with Tom until the small hours of Sunday morning. He told them he was going to stay in the hotel too, to see that they were alright and to make it easier for them to talk to him whenever they felt like it.

He tried to relax them that first night, having decided not to try for anything substantial yet, let them settle in and like him a little bit before that. He told them stories from the paper, ordinary office antics they could smile stiffly at as they got the first few drinks down, stuff he was inventing as he said it, or pranks half-recalled from school rapidly repurposed to try and raise a laugh. Richard's rigidity eased. He had barely spoken but appeared in fair humour, nodding along amicably as he downed his whiskies. John watched him drink. In the middle of one of Tom's endless monologues, Carmel said, You talk a lot, don't you?

He admitted that he did. I've always been like that but I've got worse since being at the paper. It's become a habit that I'm always recording everything I see and then describing it later. Sometimes I forget that everything which occurs in life isn't going to be written up.

What did you see when you met us? she asked. How would you describe us?

Tom laughed diffidently, trying to mask his discomfort and gauge her. She hadn't spoken enough yet for him to have a grasp on how stupid or otherwise she was, if she was asking an angry question or an innocent one.

Well, I'd like to have met you all under different circumstances of course. But as things are, what I see are three people clearly in a lot of shock, in a lot of pain, who don't know the truth about what happened, and who are desperately worried about Lucy right now.

He hoped he was right to have gambled on sincerity.

50

Is that true? Carmel asked him, and he knew that he hadn't been right at all. You wouldn't describe us as knackers, or gypsies? Or thieves and liars? Or even just Paddies? And would you not call Lucy a murderer? Worse than that, a murderer of a child, a little toddler? And if Lucy was doing that at her age, surely you'd say she had to learn her evil off someone, somewhere, probably off her family? Would you not describe us that way?

I wouldn't, he protested.

I'm only taking the mickey out of you, relax, she said, I couldn't give a shit what you see us as or what you call us. We're here because we've no money and nowhere else to go, you know that and we know that. Don't think I'm a fool, that's all I'm saying. It doesn't matter what you say about it because in a few days this will all be over and the truth will come out and Lucy will be back home and then we'll sue the police for ten thousand pounds. So I hope you write all about that as well, I hope you describe it beautifully.

He wasn't at all surprised to hear a little fussing, a little backlash like this one – hardly anyone except the really criminally thick believed that a journalist was helping them out from goodness. The interesting thing to see was how cool she remained as she delivered her blow. He was impressed by her again, this girl who wasn't much older than twenty-five and whose young daughter she had just seen accused of society's gravest crime.

Almost anyone would have had some kind of breakdown by now, but she seemed untouchable. He wondered what would happen to her in private, if there would be some inevitable collapse of facade when she locked her door later. She wasn't drinking with the fervour of her brother nor with the steadiness of her dad. She sipped on glasses of shandy indifferently. It seemed unlikely that drink would be the way of getting into her. This made his heart glad, for he liked the thought of an unusual challenge, liked the thought of himself having to access the methods of shrinks and priests instead of strictly working from the playbook of hacks. Still, it was best not to risk any serious friction now, before they started.

I don't think you a fool, he assured her, but then we don't know each other at all yet. I hope we'll change that in the morning. I'd like to talk to you all one-on-one for a little while, once you've had the chance to get a good sleep in and adjust to the new surroundings. I've arranged for some clothes and basics to be sent round first thing, they'll be left outside your doors.

He made sure to say that he arranged these things rather than saying that the paper had arranged them. No matter how canny or suspicious Carmel might turn out to be, he knew it was possible to disassociate himself from the publication he worked for on a moment-by-moment basis if he worked at it. Most people, particularly those caught in a dire moment of confusion with a need for comfort, were more or less incapable of feeling the true weight of the paper which lay behind his pleasant individual presentation. Most people like that, severed from the past and all their coping mechanisms, needed only the feeling of one person seeming to like and respect them.

Now, I'm off to bed. Breakfast is until eleven. Goodnight – it's been a terrible day for you I know, but I hope it was the worst one you'll have and things look brighter soon.

The three sat in silence without looking at one another until they heard his footsteps trail into silence up the stairs. John cleared his throat. A tension which hadn't existed when Tom was at the table solidified and took hold. There was a feeling of embarrassment.

We need to agree a plan, said John finally.

What are you on about? Carmel asked, shaking her head. We don't need a plan because we haven't done anything. And neither has Lucy. So there's nothing to be afraid of.

There's plenty to be afraid of. If we were angels there would still be plenty to be afraid of here, and I think it's fair to say we aren't that, do you? Do you Carmel?

You're a stupid old man. Nobody cares about anything I've done, or Richie, or you. There's plenty you've done you should be ashamed of, but they won't care about that, although maybe they should. We're nobody. Do you think newspapers are interested in who slept with whose wife and who drinks too much and who had an argument over land thirty years ago? They only care about who murdered Mia, and it wasn't Lucy, so we've nothing to hide.

I'm not saying I think Lucy did it—

Good! shouted Carmel.

But it doesn't matter what I think about it. The fact is that if they charge Lucy, they'll rake up every detail about us and about her. They'll go back to Waterford and talk to every Tom, Dick and Harry on the street there who ever exchanged two words with us. And then, Carmel, if God forbid they find her guilty, they'll put it on the front page of every newspaper and all of our lives will be ruined, including yours, including Lucy's.

And Mia's, said Richard.

What? John said sharply, turning to his son.

Mia is dead. Neither of you seem to know that. Or care if you do.

Says the fellow who was roused from the toilet bowl to be told they'd found her. The fellow who didn't even know she was missing until she was dead. The only man of able body in the whole estate who didn't go out looking for her? said John.

Richie shook his head, sulkily, in a way which was mildly uncanny for a man of his age.

Be that as it may, it seems pretty lousy that all you two are thinking about are yourselves, when there's a little girl

53

who's lost her life and her family at home in bits tonight not knowing what happened to her.

Well Richie I'm delighted you dragged your head out of the trough long enough to comment on matters, but actually it's Lucy we're concerned about right now. Of course it's a disgrace what happened to Mia, and she was a dote, but they've to find who actually did it. And in the meantime, my child is being accused of something she didn't do, said Carmel.

He was stung by the unfairness of it all, Carmel and his father ganging up on him and getting on the moral high horse – them!

Your child? Your child, since when Carmel? I'd say this might be the first time in history you've said those two words. She might have come out of you, but she was Rose's child as well you know, and she's nobody's child any more. She's only your child now because you're excited by the drama, finally something to distract you from the big fucking show you made of yourself and your life, finally a chance to be the centre of attention again just like you've always thought you deserve to be. Something to draw on if you ever get back to your am-dram class – except that it was Mia's father who taught it wasn't it? Wouldn't think you'll be welcomed back there any time soon.

I fucking hate you, Carmel said to him.

Well I fucking hate you both, Richard replied.

At the top of the stairs, Tom listened.

Part III

Part III

1.
CARMEL
Waterford, 1978

Some of the first warnings of pregnancy were not unlike the physical markers she had experienced when falling in love. There was the gaping feeling in her chest which swooped in without warning and winded her. There was a vague nausea and dread at all times. There was the comically heightened emotional life, everything living just on the surface so that the sight of a puppy or the news of someone she had never met having a stroke could make her burst into tears.

(On a bus to the seaside one day a woman asked an old man to move his bag so she could sit down. The old man was on his own and the woman asked this a little abrasively. He seemed unhappy and said, I have some drinks in my bag I'd like to have to hand, and the woman didn't respond, waiting him out, and he sighed and put the bag between his feet. The woman sat down, rolling her eyes. Why had this exchange made her so deeply miserable?)

She had fallen in love when she was sixteen years old. It was only a few months since her first kiss when it happened. She did not fall in love with the recipient of the first kiss, a sweaty fellow named Brian, who she embraced behind the cinema surrounded by jeering friends. One of the friends had his dog Helen out with him and when Brian's lips finally touched hers – relief! The end of the teasing, the end of being frigid – a boy picked up the chocolate Labrador named after his dead granny and threw it at them. Carmel told Richie this later that night in the room they shared when he came back home.

I don't know what you mean, Carmel. What do you mean they threw a dog at you? he whispered in the darkness.

I'm telling you what I mean, he picked up the dog and threw it at us, she said, and they both fell into helpless laughter.

Carmel liked it when Richie was staying. They had enjoyed sharing a room when he still lived at home, even though they complained about it. There were things to discuss always, and despite the five years between them they could ask one another questions about the opposite sex, trying to gain some insight where they had none; Carmel worried that her speaking voice was too low, but he assured her that boys didn't like when a girl was all squeaky and high-pitched; Richie mentioned that he seemed to have stopped growing around five feet eight and wondered if this would be a handicap, but she told him he might grow more still and if he didn't that was fine because he was taller than loads of girls so he'd just have to go with one of them.

Between the time of Carmel's first kiss and when she fell in love, Richie had gone again, leaving their house on Mayor's Walk for a friend's sofa in Ballybeg. There had been a row with their father, or rather one of many, the habitual bickering had become too much to tolerate. Usually when Richie went suddenly, without letting her know first or telling her where to find him, she fretted. This time, though, there was already too much to be considering – and, she thought ruefully, she couldn't have told Richie about what was happening anyway. They couldn't have whispered about it together in the night, because Richie knew him, and he wasn't only as old as Richie but two years beyond that again.

On Saturdays Carmel helped her mother, Rose, do the deep-clean shift at the primary school, and on Sundays she used the money to go to the pictures at the Regina cinema on Patrick Street. Sometimes she worried that her mother might take offence to the fact she never invited her, but when she confessed this guilt she was told not to be silly.

It's your money to do what you want with and your time as well, love, she said, I use mine to have a drink with Lorna, and I don't invite you to that, do I?

She did not, although sometimes Carmel would be still up in the kitchen when the two of them came back from the Old Castle half-cut and laughing and coming in for a nightcap. Her mother would pour her one too and she enjoyed the cosy feeling of it burning through her chest as she sat with them and listened to them talking shit about everyone unfortunate enough to have fallen beneath their gaze that evening.

And so Carmel was free to do as she liked those Sunday mornings, leaving with a smile at her mam clattering around the kitchen moaning about her sore head. She loved the feeling of doing something on her own, and doing it in a routine. It felt thrillingly adult and affirmed her most cherished hope, the hope that she might have an actual inner life of substance and note. It was hard to feel like that in the house sometimes. There she had minimal privacy, her father barging in whatever room he felt like when he got bored and ratty, or else there was a row on, or it was her turn to cook.

School was scarcely better. She loved her friends and it was at times relaxing to feel like part of a gang, but with them too there seemed always to be some drama or accusation unfolding which she had to take a stance on and get involved with. There was little time to dig into herself, to try to confirm the suspicion which had been growing in her recently that she might be interesting. At school sometimes

59

she locked herself in a toilet and wrote in her diary and used her compact mirror to investigate different parts of herself. There were those stolen probing moments, and there was her weekly cinema outing, where she submerged herself beneath her big flamboyant emotions and communed with the actresses, trying to feel as swept up in the parts as they were.

Alright, Carmel? Derek O'Toole said to her every week as he sold her the ticket. What are you in for today?

And they smiled at one another as she told him.

Derek was the older brother of one of Richie's best friends and had occasionally knocked in to Mayor's Walk to call for him when Richie still lived at home. Carmel hadn't thought much about him back then when she was only a kid, but she could see now that Derek was handsome, with his dark curling hair worn a little bit long but not a mess like some of the others, and a trim moustache and kind blue eyes. She liked that he was usually reading. Sometimes she would ask him what it was and they'd have a chat about it before she went in to the film. When she saw him out the odd time, walking around town with his friends or on the rare occasions she was in the pub, she thought he seemed nicer than the usual crowd.

He didn't shout, neither at his friends nor at girls they'd pass. He seemed to be listening to people when they spoke to him which was, she thought, a sad rarity in boys. His little brother and Richie were always screaming over one another hysterically and putting on a big show if they felt someone else watching, but Derek didn't have that same mugging desperation which was so common. He didn't treat her like a baby or like he had to try it on with her. The first few times she encountered him at the cinema she dreaded speaking to him, bracing herself in case he made her feel stupid, but now they were almost friends.

On the Sunday she saw *Watership Down*, she left the

cinema still streaming tears and her chest heaving. She pulled her red woollen hat low as she emerged, embarrassed but enjoying the way it wasn't easy to stop, the way her brain kept loading its sadness back up in a wave when she tried to calm down.

Have you been in the wars, Carmel? Derek shouted over at her, grinning.

He was putting on his brown leather jacket, shift finished.

She laughed through it and wiped her face and said, Oh, it's just – and then she had another wave as she thought of trying to explain and began crying all over again.

Hey, alright youngwan, you're alright. Here come back into the office with me while I get my smokes, and he ushered her through the staff door.

She sat on a swivel chair with her face in her hands, mortified and tentatively appreciating the attention. Once he had found his cigarettes he bent down and parted her hands and gave a stiff pat to the bobble on her foolish hat.

You're always crying, he said, what has you crying every other week? You can't be that soft. Is something else going on?

No, no, she said, and found that she was holding onto one of his hands, this is the only place anything goes on. I've no life. It helps me get it out of my system, do you know what I mean?

I know what you mean. I'm the same with my books sometimes, I have a cry at a character dying, but it's one I've been saving up a long time. Is it that way for you?

That's it exactly, she said and sighed with satisfaction, getting the last breath of the crying jag out of her.

I won't worry, so, he said, and he bent in awkwardly and gave her nose a kiss before he straightened up, releasing his hand from hers.

She loved him then, and smiled to let him know.

2.

The six days between her falling in love and seeing him again passed with beautiful agonising length. Her diary came alive. For years it had mostly contained despairing condemnations of her family members and dull recounting of her friendships' vagaries, followed by general summations of how disappointing her life was as a whole, but something had happened now, and she felt the great expanse of the blank pages before her like a promise of all that would follow.

'Derek O'Toole kissed me today! I mean, not really. He didn't kiss me on the mouth, but I think he will the next time I see him alone. I can't believe it. I feel like I've fallen off a boring big ship I've been stuck on for my whole life and been dropped into the ocean.'

She spent the time trying to recall everything she could about him, what she had casually observed but paid no mind to in the past. She recounted in the diary the time she had seen him on the quay at the St Patrick's Day parade with his friends, when they were all pissed but he wasn't and they had started screaming IRA songs and she had seen him shake his head and roll his eyes in mock exasperation and saunter off to another group, friends of his dad's, instead. He was civilised.

She thought of Richie's eighteenth birthday in their house in Mayor's Walk, when two brothers, the Kavanaghs, her least favourite of Richie's friends, had approached Richie. They started screeching crude comments about her mother to him. They knew that Rose wasn't Richie's mother by birth, so they felt the added allowance to be disgusting about her.

Some arse on Mrs Green there, Richie, do you think so yourself? You're lucky growing up around that, boy, I can tell you, whooped Jimmy Kavanagh.

Carmel had watched this, seen Jimmy pour himself out a glass of punch as he did it, punch that Rose had made earlier that day with Carmel's help. She had sliced the oranges. Richie was too nervous to say anything back to the Kavanaghs, and Carmel didn't hate him for it but it made her feel worried for him, and sick for herself because that was her mother they were talking about, and she was only next door at Lorna's.

Richie sniggered and said, Ah give over lads will you, and turned away.

But they kept on.

Joey Kavanagh said, I'd say you made a mess of yourself a few nights at bathtime did you Richie?

And the two brothers bent over laughing together at his discomfort.

Derek had been sitting in an armchair near to where Carmel stood in the corner, watching it all. He stood up, and grasped Joey by the back of his neck, firmly but without malice, like a mother cat.

He drew his head closer, while Joey yelped, Fuck off!

Don't you two sad little pricks ever speak like that again about a woman in her own house, he said, standing a good foot taller than Joey, looking into Jimmy's eyes as he said it, And not in front of her children. You can save the filth for when you're home in your own shithole.

He let him go and moved away from them both, waiting in the kitchen until they had left. Then he had come out and said happy birthday again to Richie and gone on his way.

Thinking of this incident recalled suddenly the knowledge that his own mother was dead. She had died long ago and Carmel could picture his little brother Colm, the one who was friendly with Richie, sitting red-eyed at their kitchen table with a glass of Coke the day after the funeral. It was a frightening, unnatural-seeming death she now remembered, nothing like the sad and ordinary kind which made up the usual neighbourhood discussions. She must only have been in her thirties and had a mysterious sort of cancer which seemed to embarrass people somehow, and she had refused to go in and stay overnight in hospital until the very end. Carmel remembered her mother describing her as rotting away in the bedroom in their house in Kilcohan, in a disapproving tone which made it sound like dying was a foolhardy experimental path Mrs O'Toole had chosen.

This fact and the way it had arrived, whole, as though from nowhere, made Carmel feel shocked and tender. It went back and changed everything; his chivalrous defence of her own mother, the nature of his devotion to and absorption in books, and certainly the magnitude and profundity of the crying he had referred to in the cinema office. How stoic he was and how unbearable she must have appeared to him, wailing about a cartoon. She loved him all the more now. His sensitivity and studiousness was not just appealing but heroic, born of suffering. All this she wrote to herself, along with descriptions of potential outfits and varying opening statements she could make when she finally saw him again.

3.

The friendship which grew between them took three months to lead to a kiss, a real one, not directed at the nose or forehead. The first day she had returned after falling in love with him, she walked down the hill to the cinema working herself up into a state, wondering if she had imagined or exaggerated the degree of intimacy which was present between them. She reprimanded herself for ruining the best part of her week, she surely couldn't bear to go in there Sunday after Sunday if he had no interest in her. God, what he must think of her – always, always on her own. For all he knew she hadn't a friend in the world. She would have to start to bring boys in with her just to get to see the films, so as not to be humiliated before him.

But when she walked in, short of breath and tight in the chest from anxiety, she knew she had not been mistaken. She was right to love. He looked over at her and was not just full of joy at the sight of her but anxious too.

I love you Derek O'Toole, she thought firmly, pressing the words, which felt tangible and sturdy, out toward him.

Here's my favourite misery guts, he said, what is it to be this week, *Our Lady of Sorrows*?

I think I'll go to *Superman*, please, Derek, she said beaming at him, I need a laugh.

He seemed pleased to hear this and said to her, Isn't that a better solution than driving yourself into a mania every week? I might even go in and watch one with you one of these days if you keep that attitude up.

Afterwards he had waited for her in the lobby and they walked out together.

He leaned against the railing while he laced up a shoe and looked at her from beneath his curly fringe and said, I've to go and visit my Nanny today, but next week I'll bring us out a cup of tea from the office and we can take it to the park for a chat if you like?

I would like that, she said to him, and they were off.

*

Why won't you kiss me? she asked him in February, sitting on their bench in People's Park facing the bandstand.

She had grown brave from the endurance of their friendship, and the increased frequency, meeting now on Wednesday afternoons as well as Sundays. She took courage also from the new frankness which had come into their conversations. He had told her about his first girlfriend, who had broken his heart, and she listened with the poised

65

sanguinity of a girl who wasn't boiling inside. She had nothing on that end to report, although she raised a laugh from the story of herself and Brian having the Labrador launched at them.

She told him the secrets she did have, about what it was like in the house in Mayor's Walk. She told him about how worried she was for Richie. The excess with which he drank seemed no longer dismissible as boyish folly. The sweet openness he had always managed to maintain despite the worst of his father's oppression had receded now into something wincing and fading. A glaze had fallen over him, one it was becoming harder to see the real Richie behind, even when he wasn't actually drunk. It was difficult to explain everything which had come before this point, the way their father spoke to Richie and didn't speak to Carmel, the way he occasionally went missing for days at a time.

After one of his disappearances, Katie in Carmel's French class said to her with satisfaction, I saw your father in Ballinaneeshagh graveyard at the weekend, Carmel. Pissed, he was.

After this it occurred to Carmel that the disappearances were every year or two and must be the anniversary of somebody's death.

She told Derek these things, and he sometimes held her cold hand in his as she spoke. This was another reason she had grown brave and manipulative.

Why won't you kiss me, Derek? Am I not pretty enough for you? she asked, knowing this was not the reason.

He snorted and rolled his eyes. Do you really think that, Carmel?

I don't know. Not really, but I can't think of why else you're so happy to talk to me, and be so close to me, but not take it any further. So sometimes I think it could be that, that I'm not as good-looking as your ex or other girls you know.

She studied him as she spoke, as alert and shrewd as she had ever been. Even this part, the preamble and bargaining, made her feel alive and quick and sharp.

It's only the obvious, that you're too young for me, he said to her.

I embarrass you? she asked him.

No, it's not that. I can tell you honestly that you're too important to me to deny you. Some of the lads already give me hassle for coming here with you all the time, but I don't mind that because it's worth it to me. It's worth it to me, and, as well, I can stand to be slagged off because they're wrong. We're not doing anything bad together, anything we shouldn't do, so they haven't a leg to stand on.

I suppose I should be grateful, that you're not sitting here with a plastic bag over your head? she said.

She was teasing him but there was real anger in her too. She disliked his background management of the situation, weighing things up and doing risk-aversion with his friends. Why had she never been consulted? When was she going to have a say over what went on between them? Who was it that put him – him and all his stupid friends – in charge of who loved who?

Carmel, he said, listen to me and stop being stupid, will you? You're the most beautiful girl in town, alright? Everyone knows that. That's part of why they get on to me, because they're jealous. You're special. Not just in the way everyone is special in their own way, but actually special – you're good-looking like a pop star or an actress, not good-looking for Waterford. And you're funny and clever and special in all those ways as well. I don't know if you know these things about yourself, because I know what girls are like sometimes, but they're only facts. And as it happens I don't believe you're insecure, really, I think you're secretly a bit of a stuck-up cow underneath all your crying and moaning.

She couldn't help but laugh at this and it made her like him so much she put her hand around to the back of his neck and stroked the curls there out of pure irresistible fondness.

See, I knew it? he said smiling back at her, But I think you should be stuck-up. I think if anything you should be ten times as stuck-up as you are now, because you are better than everyone else. The rest of them only think it, and that's why it's embarrassing when you see them showing off, but you really are. That's why I can't kiss you, or go with you, because I'd have to hide it all, because of how young you are, and I couldn't bear to hide you away when you are so special.

There was no immediately obvious way to contradict this flattering logic. She faced forward, shading her eyes against the pale sun glaring right at her, wrapped the navy quilt coat around herself. She contemplated the state of things, a calm flush of pleasure passing over her. He did love her after all, so much that it wouldn't be enough for him to keep her on the side. Now that she knew that, she didn't want to wait any longer.

Well, she said, deliberating, I appreciate that. I appreciate you speaking so honestly to me. I think I must have made my feelings clear by now.

It felt to them both that she had skipped some essential moment. She had gone from never having a boyfriend, only a few tepid kisses with nobodies, to the strange emotional sophistication she seemed to now inhabit. She had missed the pivotal stage of agonising and awkwardness which usually characterised early liaisons, straight to the strikingly adult frankness she was addressing him with now.

If I haven't made my feelings clear, I love you. And I've loved you for months, and I think you love me too. So the only thing I can say is that even if people disapprove, there won't be anything wrong with it.

68

Richie will kick off when he finds out. And your father—

My father doesn't give a fuck what I do, she said coolly, but the terribly sophisticated emotional laid-bareness wore a little thin with this one. And Richie doesn't know one end of the week from the other. He'll be at our wedding in ten years not having realised we ever got together. For God's sake, it isn't like you're so ancient, you've only just gone twenty-three. And girls grow up faster than boys, even my mother says that's why things work out the way they do.

For a moment the image occurred to her of her father's prematurely ancient affect, the discoloured beard and yellow wizened teeth, and how sometimes it jarred her to look up and see him next to her mother, still rounded and smooth and well turned out, the handful of years between them screamingly apparent. But she shook it away.

I agree with you there, he said and looked like he was going to cry, kissing her knuckle twice, fiercely and briefly. Do you mean you'll wait for me, if that's what we have to do?

I will if you will, she said, but I don't think it would hurt to get a little bit of practice in so we're ready when the time comes, and turned to him with everything shining behind her, the sun lighting her hair from its usual black into blue and red, and kissed him.

4.

They didn't, in the end, wait for her birthday. Their mutual willingness to do so seeming sufficient. They found their ways, instead. Derek shared a dingy flat on Manor Street with a sad divorced man named Andy who was in his forties and worked nights in the Bausch & Lomb factory. A few days a week they had several hours between when he left for work and when Carmel would be missed at home. As it happened her mother didn't give her a hard time even when

69

she did come home late, because she had always been a good girl. She wanted this to be kept up, so she was home by ten, telling stories of being at Nicole's house or at the pictures.

Nobody questioned these things, and there was no reason for them to. Sometimes the lies made her feel even lonelier than usual when she got into bed at the end of them, pressing herself up against the cool wallpaper and failing to feel her body as anything material, it was lost in the darkness of her home as it always was. And the hours were lost to history. If Derek died she would be the only one who knew about them. Thinking this made tears spring to her eyes. She had to think back to every part of him to make her body less lonely and more purposeful, how red his mouth got, much redder than hers, after they kissed for a long time.

She surprised herself by not feeling nervous to be naked in front of him. She believed what he told her about how rare and perfect she was, and assumed correctly that his beliefs would apply to her body also. She was fascinated by the new use of her sturdy frame, previously good for gymnastics and running for buses, and how powerful it was. They moved quickly, fluidly together, and she wondered if this was why anybody really wanted to be athletic, surely this could be the only possible point of it all.

One night in the blue light of the street lamp outside, both of them still breathless and perspiring, she was fiddling with his hair, burying her face in it, and then she started to cry.

Uh-oh, he said, what is it, love? Why are you sad?

I'm sad because I'm so happy. I love you so much and you're going to die, she said to him, I don't mean right now, although that could happen too, but someday you'll die, and I'll remember this and I won't be able to bear it.

Cheer up, Car. You could die before me, he said.

God, don't I know it. That's the only thing that keeps me going, she said, making them both laugh.

And then she said, more seriously, Will you promise to let me be the one to die first?

5.

Three months in, it was May, and they remained, to the best of their knowledge, undetected. Two times since the affair began they coincided unintentionally.

One evening Carmel had tagged along with Richie, there was a party at the pirate radio station which had been raided and moved from Kilotteran to Wellington Street, which sounded like an appealingly dangerous way to spend the night to Carmel. It was only a dozen or so men sitting around with cans and a red gel taped over the lights, the room dense with smoke and them all seriously playing Roxy Music and discussing what The Who would be like without Keith Moon. Carmel felt the familiar slump of disappointment and considered walking straight back out and not wasting sleep staying up here, but then saw Derek crouching in a corner laughing with a friend. He looked over and threw her a brief, safe wink – casual enough to be forgotten even if it was observed – and she stayed for hours, never speaking but comfortable in the warmth of their complicity.

Not long after, she had called in one afternoon to what was fondly described as the Hippie Commune in John's Park, a sitting room populated by a handful of handsome Jethro Tull fans smoking hash and holding forth on philosophy and the issues of the day – sent by her father to track down Richie after he hadn't been heard from in some days and a fine for public nuisance had arrived at the house. She knocked shyly on the window and waved at the men, who looked back at her with benevolent blankness.

'Richie?' she said softly, miming it and shrugging to

indicate her question, and then Derek came into view, laughed and shook his head to say no, not here. He flapped his hand to say go away, but in a friendly amused way which only meant it was funny to see her in this place.

Aside from those brief interludes, they kept themselves to Derek's apartment. Carmel sometimes had to disrupt the sex-and-then-dinner routine they had fallen into, to study for her Fifth Year exams. She sat up in his bed with the books in her lap and cupped her hands to shield her eyes from his body. His body lay the other way, feet up beside her and head dangling off the end of the mattress. He held a novel aloft to read from. They had come to this arrangement to minimise the chance of them distracting one another. When she suggested that she just study at home if they weren't going to really be together on these nights, he looked offended and she loved him for it. She knew herself why it was worth it, why they couldn't waste the chance to be near each other even when they couldn't speak or touch.

She left feeling contented and that the studying meant more than studying done at other times. The hours weighty and golden, the knowledge embedded with particular significance. Their reading in tandem made her think with fondness and something like nostalgia for the future about a time when they'd live together in Dublin and sit in their living room like this. Turning pages, putting out the other hand to touch the other person's every so often. There were never children in her thoughts of the future.

One night after they'd finished eating, he reached out and pulled her chair towards him. He had been quiet during the meal and she felt a tense ache in her stomach. She had been unwell for a few days.

I've to tell you something, he said.

He looked excited now, and she wondered with relief if

he might take her away for a night, or even book in a dinner in town for the night of her birthday when they could go official.

I got an offer of a job in Dublin. In a library, Carmel. An old friend of my mother runs the one in Rathmines and she called in to my father's house a few months back. We got chatting and she saw what a reader I am and that I'm stuck doing nothing in Waterford except standing behind the desk and scrubbing the toilets in the Regina.

She tried to take it in, what he was telling her. She kept smiling broadly at him as he spoke and she smoothed it out in her mind. It was a shock but it wouldn't be too bad. Once they were open about the relationship in a few short weeks, they could alternate visiting on weekends. She said as much to him, after he had stopped rabbiting on about this damned library. Stupid woman, she was, uprooting him before they were ready to leave together. But it was making him happy, she saw, and anyway—

It won't be too long, really, will it, love? she said, and tried to match his level of excitement.

What won't, darling? he asked her.

When I can come up to join you. I'll come up straight after I finish the Leaving Cert next year, I won't even wait the summer I don't think. I'll definitely get into college somewhere in Dublin.

He cocked his head, and held the side of her face. And that was when he explained that he didn't think it would be fair on either of them to have a whole year not being together. It wouldn't be possible for her, with her Leaving Cert to study for, or for him trying to settle down and make a life and friends for himself in Dublin. It was beautiful what they had shared together these last few months, but it had naturally come to an end now with this new chapter in his life. And that was it, that was the end of everything.

6.

She went in to the cinema on a night she knew he wasn't working, hoping to feel some of the old power it had to absorb or match her grief. She lasted only five minutes before she had to burst out of her seat, sweating with nausea. It was the baby inside her, about eight weeks old now, and the smell of the popcorn. For the rest of her life she would hate the smell of cinema popcorn.

Carmel had been on holidays from school for three weeks, having clumsily fumbled through the exams into mediocre results, when she discovered she was pregnant. She had never menstruated with complete regularity, so it wasn't the missed periods which alarmed her to begin with. It was a strange, tight gassiness she hadn't experienced before, which extended sometimes into her chest when she ate. She felt feverish and lethargic and welled up with obscure emotion all the time, but she ascribed these maladies to her missing Derek (both the sadness and the hot little engine of anger she could feel gearing toward him; she thought darkly in the dead of night of how she might ruin his life by telling everyone what they had been doing before his great escape to Dublin).

The first dim alarm began to sound when one morning she woke barely able to pull on a jumper, so tender and painful were her breasts. The discomfort lasted into the afternoon, when a memory of something her mother's friend Lorna had grumbled about surfaced in the shallows of her consciousness. Hadn't she said how sore she was there once, when she was pregnant with Becky? The thought took up maddening residency on the outer edges of her mind, an impossibility that could not be dismissed. After three days of internal bickering she forced herself to go to the library on a Friday. She searched with great discretion for a book about biology and pregnancy and scoured the symptoms list. There in a straightforward litany was every feeling which had passed through her body for the last month. She wadded up the raggedy ink-blotted sleeve of her uniform jumper and took it into the bathroom to inspect.

Then it was true. The knowledge was too enormous and unthinkable, she wasn't able to stand under it and as quietly as she could she slid down the cool wall. She put two fingers to the flighty pulse in her throat, pressing hard against it and overcome by the idea she was pumping blood into what would be a child. It was a terrible thought. She wanted immediately to block off her arteries and blood cells and oxygen altogether rather than let it continue. At home she got straight into bed and explored herself. She pushed from the outside of her stomach up and in where she felt her womb might be. She tested her breasts and tried to see where they hurt the most, around the nipple and under her armpits. She put her fingers inside her vagina as far as they would go, to see what knowledge they could grope there. She cried with frustration at the darkness she was touching, no idea what it was exactly or what any of it meant.

For a few minutes she allowed herself to imagine telling Derek and getting him back. It was doubtful a fellow like him would go so far as to deny her after this. It was more likely to be the case that he would be pragmatic and bite the bullet, move back to Waterford and get a different job and marry her. His idea of himself wouldn't allow anything else, he wouldn't be able to bear dishonour. But she didn't want to be the bullet that got bitten. She didn't want to be the breeding, nagging witch who got him back through the natural sublimity of conception. She reddened with humiliation and rage at the thought of him reluctantly packing up his groovy little studio flat and kissing goodbye whatever silly women he was probably having cappuccinos with in

Dublin. Of him greeting her with a stoic smile, a martyred will to make the best of a bad situation.

Well, she wasn't a bad situation. She wouldn't be made into one. It was Derek himself who had given her confidence, and even though he had left her he hadn't managed to take with him the tenuous infrastructure he had built inside her, when he convinced her she was more special and beautiful and interesting than anyone else. She wasn't the sort of girl who wheedled a man into coming home to half-love her in joint misery as long as they both shall live. She'd show him that one day. She would get past all this and be the better woman for it. She would do amazing things in her life, be on the stage and write songs and marry someone genius and ten times as handsome as Derek. She promised this to herself fervently in the desperation of that first night alone with her secret. And there was even some part of her which felt excited by how disastrous her situation was. She was looking forward in a way to whatever sleight of hand she would figure out to resolve it, and it was by far the most dramatic and definitively narrative thing to have happened to her since she had fallen in love.

Over the next week, her mind felt clear and dynamic in the face of urgency. She was often good in the immediate aftermath of a crisis, quick to distract her father when he had begun a fight, or to clean up Richie's vomit swiftly before anyone else woke. She knew from the book in the library that it could only be tiny now, a little grape or a nut. She thought of it with scorn, as an unworthy adversary. It had barely even begun, it must be easy to get rid of it at this stage. She just had to dislodge it from where it had stuck to her. When she bled after she'd done it, it wouldn't even be like the end of a real pregnancy, but only a late period coming on at last.

At first she thought vigorous movement would be enough. She put on her PE kit and ran for miles down the

76

Cork Road until she felt she would vomit, and while doubled over in that state, panting and wild, she punched herself in the stomach where she thought it would be. Following a few fruitless days of this, her panic began to grow, it was pushing up against her skull and threatening to splinter. She knew of the rumoured old wives' tales that were supposed to bring it on. There had been two girls who got pregnant since she had started at the Ursuline convent. Both of them disappeared when they started to show and never came back to school. One got married and the other left Waterford and moved to England. Nobody knew if she kept the baby.

Carmel didn't know anyone who had had an abortion, either the legitimate sort in England nor the hushed-up frightening sort girls whispered about. But she knew that hot baths and gin were something, though not why those things in combination might work. She knew also in a very distant way something about a wire coat hanger, and this part was even more opaque in her imagination, it was too monstrous and strange a thought so that it barely felt like a real thing people did and more like an urban legend, a big forbidding skull and crossbones over the idea of abortion.

She did not care about abortion, or had never thought of it much one way or another. Even now fixed in her grim all-consuming determination to rid her body of its scourge she didn't relate to it as an issue to be argued over or spoken of. The distance between those arguments and the physical materiality of her desire seemed unbroachable. There was no thought in her urge, and it seemed not to have to do with anything that had ever happened in history before, to any other person. That it must be made to leave her body was so obvious and necessary that there was no way to verbalise it, not even in the privacy of her own head.

*

On Saturday she told Rose that she felt unwell and couldn't come to help with her cleaning. On the radio, Blondie sang and Carmel thought of the party in the radio station, of looking at Derek from a distance and how it was pleasurable then, how the distance was permanent now and would hold no pleasure again.

She stole a bottle of dusty gin from her mother's area of the drinks cupboard, sniffing it to make sure Richie hadn't watered it down to nothing, and locked the door of the bathroom. She ran the bath as hot as it would go, sitting on the edge of it drinking the gin in foul gulps as it filled up. She let out a guttural growl of pain as she lowered herself in, thinking, to make her continue: Imagine how much more painful it would be to have a baby.

In the scalding water she trembled with shock and drank as quickly as she could. She had never been able to drink much and had to keep pressing her hand to her mouth and pausing to let her body accept it without regurgitating. After an hour she had gotten through the bottle and the water had started to cool and she didn't feel anything happening. She put her fingers inside herself, trying to open something up, but she did not know what she was doing. She was far drunker than she had ever been, and started to cry. Why was nothing moving? She climbed out of the bath unsteadily, black spots flashing in her vision. She wrapped a towel around herself and went to the bedroom for the hanger she had hoped she would not need. She topped up the bath with more hot water and climbed back in, straightening the sharp end of the wire into an implement of the sort she thought it should be.

Under the water, she tried to open herself again with one hand, and gingerly began to insert the wire with the other. She moved it, trying to find some purchase or area where it felt it could gain access. She took a deep breath, ready to commit great pain against herself. But there was nothing.

All she was met with was resistance, and now she cried because it was the end of the world. She cried with appalled hatred for the way of her body, that the thing was so tiny and so inconsequential and so proximate, and yet could not be reached. She had exhausted the hope and anger which had fuelled her. The wire jabbed uselessly against some part of her body that seemed to have no give at all. If she were to try to tear through this she would be gambling on destroying herself entirely, and she knew that she was not willing to do so. If she grievously wounded herself, even if the pregnancy ended, everyone would know what had happened, and what was driving her was the need for privacy. What was driving her was the need for no other person on earth to ever find out what was taking place inside her body. In this, she had failed.

Many hours later, having vomited and slept through the worst of her drunkenness, a moment of clarity came to her like a miracle through the fog of her despair, a last burst of conviction that she would simply not allow this to take place. She would stop eating. She would starve the thing out.

She lasted five days with no food at all and hardly any water. She spent the first two walking in purposeful circles around the park, before realising such activity could not be sustained on air. Then she took to her bed almost entirely, where she thought of St Catherine of Siena, who had stopped eating as an act of refusal when her parents insisted she marry her dead sister's widower. She didn't want to marry anyone or to ever bear children, she wanted something different and more important for herself instead. She would only eat Eucharist, and glided through her short brilliant life fuelled by the power of her faith and will. When Carmel made brief appearances outside her room, her mother asked what she was doing in there and if she was unwell, and Carmel smiled benevolently and said she was only reading.

Will we go to the cinema the two of us Carmel, you haven't been out in ages have you? asked Rose, a little worried through her general air of distracted busyness.

We can, Mam, but not until next week, okay? I'm just trying to get through some stuff this week.

For school, like? I know you were very disappointed in your results but it was only a wobble, you got nervous. It's the Leaving Cert that counts anyway.

I know, it'll be fine next year. And we'll go to the cinema on Monday.

By Sunday she had stopped thinking about food at all and felt celestially high and comforted and hollowed-out. She hadn't bled yet but there was no doubt in her mind that she had achieved what she had meant to, impossible that the dirty wretched thing had survived the purity of this devotional fast. It had to be this way, so that she could prove to herself what she was willing to sacrifice for the big life she wanted and was owed. Falling into a delirious sleep that night something clicked in her mind. It was enabled by both the fact of her starvation and the fact she had never taken a pregnancy test, never actually seen any verifiable proof. The mind clicked and Carmel no longer believed in her pregnancy. It no longer existed; except physically, except in reality.

7.

God you've gotten awfully fat, Carmel, in the face, her mother said to her in late July. It suits you, though, and you've got boobs at last.

Carmel smiled.

She had asked her mother for whatever shifts she could spare during the summer, and had ended up with four days a week in the hospital because another cleaner had broken

80

her hip. She worked with manic vigour. She started going to the cinema again, without eating anything. She still was conscious of not giving the baby-thing any nourishment, even though she also didn't believe in its existence.

Her breasts stretched through their papery encagements so she stopped wearing them.

She was fat, but, so what? Lots of girls were fat.

She began to drink. Her eyes receded, watery, red, into her face which had always been so sharp and pale.

She tried to join in with Richie a few nights, to make it feel social and pleasant instead of curative. She hadn't met these new friends of his. They frightened her in a vague way, they didn't like her, and didn't seem to like Richie very much either. The way they drank was cruel, and hyper-active. If a bottle ended then it had to be replaced from somewhere, no matter how it was obtained. They had to go to someone's parents' house, or a bar one of them worked in, and get enough so that nobody was desperate any more.

In August Carmel was drinking a bottle of wine a day, sipping it from morning until bedtime, because she found her nerves were able to steady that way. And when she went to sleep it was too cloudy to have to think of anything. In the morning she tucked the empty bottle into her under-wear as she left the house and threw it in the nearest place she could find.

Her face had ballooned. Her body hadn't changed that much. She ate nothing except two pieces of toast in the morning.

One morning she woke up and felt something move in her stomach. She found a belt and fastened it around her middle as tight as it would go. Then she put on her clothes over that, and went on to her cleaning job, her mother cry-ing briefly about the teenager killed in the IRA attack on Lord Mountbatten, and quickly shutting up when her father glared meaningfully at her for her weakness.

81

8.

There was a morning in September when Rose had asked
something of her, which she never did. She had asked if
Carmel might come to the anniversary Mass of Rose's
mother, in the Sacred Heart. It had been ten years since she
had died. Carmel woke up late and was panic-stricken, fum-
bling around her room for clothes, and she did hear, dimly,
a thundering on the stairs, but she didn't register it, not as
something important.

Then her mother burst in the door, just at the worst time,
just as Carmel was lifting a dress over her head so that
everything was on full show.

Jesus Christ, Carmel, her mother said.

What? said Carmel. She didn't feel any panic yet, just
annoyance.

Rose closed the door behind her, and sat on the bed.

What? she said again, I'll only be two minutes.

Carmel, her mother repeated, Carmel. She was crying
then. Carmel, you're pregnant, she said.

Carmel laughed.

And she laughed again. She was naked except for a pair of
knickers. She avoided looking into the mirror, as she had
done for months. She was suddenly extremely frightened
and wanted to be alone.

No, I'm not, Mam. It doesn't matter. Just go downstairs
and I'll see you in a minute.

Rose was doubled over with her head between her
knees and she was moaning, My daughter, my own daughter, over and over.

Fuck off Mam please, Carmel shouted, panicking. Get
out of here, I'm begging you.

Something was happening in her head, disintegrating.

There was a wall she had built that was being taken away without her permission.

She grasped to try and find the clothes to put on, but they seemed to have been kicked away or removed. She felt around her for something to help and there was nothing. Her mother was dissolving. Her clothes had disappeared. There was nothing in the room any more, except she heard out of nowhere a slow steady thrum in her ears, and felt confused about whether she was hearing her own heartbeat or something else. Was that her, Carmel, or was it the sound of someone else in there with her? She turned, slowly, toward the mirror. She looked at herself.

She was five months pregnant. She saw that it was true. Her hand flew to her mouth, cold disgust rising in her throat, things happening behind her face, nerves burning and short circuiting and everything ending again.

9.
London

In the abortion clinic, as Rose had told her would happen, they did a scan and saw how far along she was and it was too late to get rid of it. Because of Carmel's season of denial, she was too late in the pregnancy to terminate. She smiled wanly when they said this, having for the moment lost the ability to care about what would happen to her or anybody else. The two women doctors or nurses seemed to viscerally hate her, and she could understand why. It wasn't just that she was an idiot, or a person who was smiling inappropriately. They hated her because she came to them asking to kill a baby which was already moving in her and because she had come from Ireland to do it.

In the waiting room earlier she had stolen a moment of

eye contact, shared shame, with a young woman with a Cork accent, and felt sullied by their communal failure. She had the impulse to apologise to everyone else, even the women there also getting terminations but who had the good grace to at least be from England. If you had the bad luck to be from Ireland, it felt, you had to suck it up and never have sex or else have the baby. To be both Irish and unwantedly pregnant was unspeakable, wrong in a way that went beyond law.

Because of how amazingly efficiently Carmel had denied the pregnancy to herself, she had never imagined what would happen now. This would be difficult to explain to other people in years to come, but it was the truth. The knowledge wasn't real to her so there had been no worst-case scenarios playing out in her head, no hypotheticals or weighing of consequences. She never thought it through one way or the other. That night in the cheap hotel near the clinic Rose and Carmel stayed in, she thought about what would come next.

You can give it up, love, Rose kept saying, but there was something that made this seem instantly and obviously impossible.

After that terrible day when her mother saw her undress, when her father found out that his daughter was pregnant, the main storyline for him was to find out who had done it. He spoke about the ghost culprit like he and Richie were going to wreak revenge on him. He was suddenly alive and vivid with spite, yanked out of his usual plodding weariness. It seemed to Carmel that he was enjoying it almost, the way the anger was directional and, it could not be denied, to do with a serious matter. His unhappiness was so encompassing and indecipherable that its usual targets were often arbitrary. This was part of what kept his misery poisonous and cyclical. He could feel the absurdity of shouting and roaring about a burnt slice of toast or a door left open and what he really wanted was a confrontation worthy of his fury. He resented Carmel denying him that. Carmel refused to tell anyone, even Rose, which made her father assume that she had secretly been leading an extensive slatternly life, that the man responsible could have been any number of men, anyone who lived in Waterford.

She kept the secret from them not out of loyalty to Derek, but because she wanted a private thought of her own. Her life was over now, she knew that. Wasn't she owed one little thing nobody else could see?

When her mother whispered to her of adoption, when she imagined birthing this baby and then giving it to some strange faceless couple, it felt entirely wrong. This was her burden; it would always be so. You couldn't say that she wanted it, but it was true that if it was going to exist, if she was forced to bring it into the world, then she couldn't live with anyone else having it either. She sorted through these feelings in the hours and days after the clinic. She felt, but couldn't say, that part of why she would never give the baby up was that it had come to feel so monstrous. It felt that Carmel had not only conceived something unwanted but then had suppressed it with such hideous madness that it could only feel something like evil to her now. It would not be right to pass on such malevolence to an innocent family.

In the hotel room in London after they were told that she must bear the baby, Carmel lay in her mother's arms weeping and said, I'm frightened, I'm so frightened.

And Rose said, doubtfully, You'll feel better once we get back home.

I'm never going back home, Carmel told her.

In the night they discussed this. Carmel told her that she couldn't bear the shame of being in Waterford pregnant, or trying to go back to school while having a baby. Rose held her child in her arms and understood, and reassured her, and even agreed in the end, in theory. Rose knew that they could stay in London, because her daft sister Fiona had a council flat she barely ever used, busy in France with her new, second husband.

It was better to begin again for everyone. A baby's arrival should be a happy time, despite the circumstances, and Rose knew she could help to look after it while Carmel got herself settled and established what she would do next.

Okay, love, said Rose, we don't have to go back. We don't have to go back, ever, if you don't want. You can start again here, and we'll help you with the baby, and it will all be fine. I'll take care of you, and there's nothing to be frightened of. You didn't do anything wrong.

But it doesn't matter even if I did, said Carmel, because we're in a different place now.

The next morning while Rose was in bed, Carmel took a bath and felt the baby fully kicking for the first time, a surge of rage as it moved against her bladder. She gritted her teeth and pressed her hands down hard and deep where she felt the movement until she cried out in pain. It was the last time she would try to hurt whatever was in there. The doctors had confirmed it – there was no separation any more, no one without the other. She was learning, in the unwanted clarity which had been thrust upon her, that she could not hurt the thing inside her without also hurting herself. She found with surprise that there was still some fragment of defiance which made her want to live.

10.

When the plan was made and for several years afterwards, Rose acted swiftly and automatically. She moved through logistics as though without thought, how you walk around familiar terrain without needing to look up or check the way. She did not give comment or opinion or insight. She intuited, as she often had before, that the family needed her blankness to absorb their chaos and questions. She brightened the blankness, turned it up and outward, making it strong and pleasantly corrosive to the doubts of others, a powerful disinfectant.

In the very first part of it when she spoke with her sister and made arrangements about keys and what to tell the neighbours, Fiona tried to press her.

What will you do in London, though, Rose? she asked. What will any of you do?

We'll get Carmel through this, and then the child will be born and we'll get the child through it.

Get the child through what? asked Fiona, tittering. What's 'it'? Do you mean life?

What's the problem if I do mean that? Rose said, hardening quickly as she had learned to do with her sisters to avoid being hurt by their derision. Somebody has to do these things, don't they?

Oh, yes, Fiona said still with her tone of garrulous wonder, everyone would have dropped dead by now if not for you. Carmel and John and Richie would be dead, I'd be dead, Connie would be dead, Mammy is dead so you must have slipped up somewhere—

Shut up Fiona you ghoul, she said, and just help me. I don't need your opinion, I just need your help. Things will work themselves out, and anyway aren't you the one who told me I needed to get out of Waterford for the last twenty years?

Yes, Fiona said, losing interest in the conversation, I think it will be good for you to try something new, I have told you that, haven't I?

Always, Rose had fixated on her own usefulness. It was a part of the urge she had to apologise for not being fully beautiful. Fiona was not beautiful either but had somehow never cared whether or not their parents liked her, had been

87

separate and scathing from the beginning. Connie was exquisite in an undeniable way which legitimised her reclusive, disdainful air. They would mock Rose when they saw the way she tried to please their parents, especially their father before he died. It was true that she behaved toward him with the nauseating servitude of another wife, a lesser, comical wife. There was something unnervingly adult and romantic about how she insisted on bringing him his slippers or making his tea. Their mother only laughed at these performances. Her sisters were openly revolted, but it made her feel comfortable to behave that way. There were other things than beauty which could be undeniable, solid gifts of service, and they helped to temper her embarrassment for existing.

She had experienced in her early forties a sense of relief when age became visible. The nearness of beauty she had previously been acutely aware of – how it bobbed just below the surface of her face where she couldn't access it, and how it shone from her sister – stopped tormenting her. Formerly it had felt akin to a personal failing, one she could overcome with an unidentified act of will or resistance never mustered. Age was something different and alien. It was separate from herself and unstoppable. It did not make her happy to see the heaviness which grew around her mouth or the slight droop of one eyelid but it was calming in its way, freeing to be looked at less as she went out in the world. When it hurt her pride she comforted herself by imagining that the varying roles of her life had been simplified, and that this was a good thing. The martryred part of her which had longed to give things to her father (and which was also, counterintuitively, a mean part of herself) found satisfaction in it.

As they prepared to hang up, Fiona asked almost as an afterthought, How do you feel about leaving Waterford? Are you angry with Carmel?

Surprised, Rose thought for a moment and said, I don't

have room to feel anything about it now, but I'm not angry, I'm sad for her. If we can do this for her, if I help her, I won't care where we are, if I can—

Well this has always been your problem, Fiona said, cutting her off. You think if you can be loved, if everyone loves you, then nothing else matters. When has that ever worked out for you?

Rose had no ready retort to this accusation, which was true. Rose was too focused to feel offended or to bother denying that this was exactly how she experienced the world. It will work out this time, when it really needs to, she thought.

When the phone call ended, she spoke to herself for a few moments. Was it true that she felt nothing? Searching herself, she couldn't find a hidden seam of fury or resentment, but noticed that there was a hint of dark excitement similar to that she had felt when each of her parents had died. It was to do with facing a task large and grave enough to make use of her pragmatism and sanity.

Two years after she first got the keys to Skyler Square, she received correspondence forwarded by their tenant in Mayor's Walk. It was a letter from the management company who looked after the graveyard her parents were buried in, letting her know that complaints had been made by the families of those buried in the neighbouring graves. The untamed shrubbery had spawned some particularly relentless and fast-moving weed which was irritating to have to keep trimming away, not to mention that it was unsightly. The letter had been received a few days previously, but Rose found it only this morning because she noticed it and some others folded up into a wedge to steady a wobbly kitchen chair. Her hands shook and a large well of sadness which she rarely looked toward opened inside of her. It was the only thing she had asked Connie for when she was preparing to leave.

Just once a fortnight is enough, she told her, to change out flowers and tidy things up. If you don't want to do it yourself then I'm sure you can pay someone else who goes there to do it for you.

Connie had bristled and looked at her sharply. She was married to a rich man who owned a chain of garden centres and she had never been employed, but was mysteriously sensitive about any acknowledgement of this difference between herself and her sisters.

Yes, she said to Rose, I think I can manage to water a plant every two weeks, thank you so much, I don't need an instruction manual.

Had she done it on purpose, Rose wondered now. Had she been insulted by the implication that she was useless and as a punishment never gone to the graves in all that time? She was shaken at the thought of the visible neglect going on without her knowledge, the idea of other families stepping around the mess, tutting. It was not a bearable shame. She regretted that she had chosen not to return for Christmas, when she could have halted this nonsense sooner.

She had asked her family if they would like to go back, but Carmel still flinched when Waterford was mentioned. John and Richie were indifferent and mumbled about money until the conversation dwindled away. She resolved to return and clean it up herself, an appropriate physical penance, and then to pay someone herself to do the upkeep going forward, if Connie couldn't do even that.

She set the letter down on the kitchen table, annoyed now at whoever it was who had so thoughtlessly wadded it up out of sight. She might never have found out. Carmel was in the bathroom, taking ages, humming something to herself as the shower went – but Rose could hear from the way the water fell that she wasn't in the shower but was doing other things and letting it run.

Carmel, she shouted, turn off the shower if you're not using it, and did you put letters under that chair? They were important.

A light scoffing came from within, and Carmel said, What was so important?

It doesn't matter, don't touch my private correspondence in future, and will you get out of there, I need to brush my teeth.

Lucy was grousing now, and Rose said, Lucy is up. Did you hear me Carmel, Lucy is up I said.

Well pick her up then, Jesus, I won't be long.

Rose went into the kitchen and took the spare brush and toothpaste she kept on the windowsill for this occurrence and began to furiously clean her teeth, grasping the sink with one hand. Carmel came in glowing and damp, still not having picked up Lucy.

I hate when you brush your teeth in here, she told Rose, It's disgusting. Spitting into the food sink. And the way you do it with your jaw wide open is rotten. I feel like I can see into your actual skull.

A darkness was passing through Rose's mind, quivering and deciding whether to spill out entirely, and then she saw that Carmel was twisting her mother's ring on her thumb. It was a valueless but pretty glass stone which held great power over Rose, remembering her mother slipping it on only on her rare nights out. It was the last thing to go on once her make-up and hair were set and the perfume on, a pleasingly pagan ritual is how it felt to Rose watching, that the night was made good and possible by the wearing of the ring.

I've asked you not to touch that, she said to Carmel, and the unusual tone in her voice shut Carmel up abruptly, she didn't try to defend herself or speak, only twisted it off and wiped it on the towel she was wearing and laid it on the kitchen table.

Do you know what we had to do for you Carmel? What I had to do? Do you never think about it at all?

Carmel turned and left the room, going to retrieve Lucy, and Rose saw that her manically strong self-preservation had kicked in. She couldn't allow it any air.

Rose felt foolish, alongside her rage. How could she tell her living child, mother of her living grandchild, that she had been forced to forsake two graves for her, and in this moment regretted it? But it was real, the confluence of abandonment and failed duty. The thought of the overgrown space which was all that remained of her parents sickened and lowered her, strongly compelled her to return. They had left her and now she had left them. That place was her home, she had no home now, and she suspected that no one would ever apologise to her for this loss.

Part IV

London, 1990

1.

On the Saturday night while her family whispered to one another, as the journalist listened, Lucy was tucked into a bed in a secure facility. She had been assigned a woman police officer to take care of her, who was kind but looked unsure and even afraid.

How long will I be here? asked Lucy.

We'll know more tomorrow, Lucy, it's just for tonight we have to keep you in this room to make sure you're safe.

Am I in jail?

The policewoman kept touching the dent above her upper lip when she wasn't certain of what to say.

It's just a place to keep you safe for the night. You don't have to be frightened. Go to sleep now and we'll get your family back in the morning to check in on you, and breakfast and nice books for you to look at until we get everything sorted out.

At the mention of her family Lucy's mouth straightened into a grim line, between a smile and sucking her teeth.

She didn't mind the feeling of the dark cell. It was small and safe and clean, almost like when she squeezed her body into the nook in the bathroom or into a cupboard at school. She couldn't see anything even when she opened her eyes, which she found peaceful. At home there was always a hum of the telly or someone talking and the lights all on. She turned in toward the cool wall, pressing her forehead against it, wrapping the blankets around herself as tight as they would go and leaning forward.

When she had hurt that boy in the playground and everyone got angry with her, all of life threatened to change in the hinge of that impulsive moment. She could feel nothing else but the enormity of it tilting over her. She remembered that week sometimes as being almost as bad as the one when Rose had died, because it felt like she had finally been found out and would be exposed.

The secret badness of her that she had always been aware of had never found a direct outlet like that one before. It was inevitable that the world would end, only then it hadn't. After a while things had gone back to normal and it was only she who still thought and talked about it often – going over to the boy and trying to speak to him, he turning away with elegant, polite coldness, or bringing it up to Carmel and asking did she think he would have a mark forever from it.

It doesn't matter now, Lucy, does it? You did it and he's alive and you won't do it again, will you?

In the cell she felt for a moment a fizzle of relief before she slept. Now at least everything really had changed, now at least the badness had come out of her and into the world and was real.

2.
Hotel Gargano, Sunday 20 May

Tom woke at six and sat at the desk to drink strong coffee and consider his strategy. It would definitely be best if they were drunk, but he couldn't wait until the evening and waste the whole day. Carmel was going to be escorted in for

96

a visit with Lucy at 10 a.m., he knew from his policeman, leaving the other two free and without her around to cluck at them or mouth off to Tom. So perhaps the best way to proceed was to get them both started early, take the old man aside once he'd loosened up a bit and see if there was anything forthcoming there.

It was difficult to know the right balance with the alcoholic – he might have such a high tolerance that he wouldn't be drunk for hours and hours, but then you didn't want to risk him reaching total incoherence if he was the sort who went from zero to one hundred without warning. Tom knew a few of those, both at home and in the paper. One of the men on the sports desk had sat next to him at the Christmas lunch and easily put away three bottles of wine, talking fine as you like, before collapsing instantly when he tried to get up to use the toilet, incapable of so much as telling the taxi driver an address once they hauled him outside. He would try Richie at 3 p.m. just in case, he decided, and John in the early evening, and Carmel straight after that, before they could speak to one another.

Tom's gut felt inflamed and swollen from the companionable drinking he'd had to do the night before and the three hours of sleep which had followed. He had a tension headache from the posed expression of benevolent worry he had maintained for those hours, eyebrows drawn in in quizzical bafflement that such terrible things could be happening to such wonderful people, mouth scrunched up to the side into a little anus of concern. His blood was racing and he felt in his body a decidedly middle-aged man's assortment of ailments. Soon would come the gout, he thought. At times it was the best thing he ever felt, the constant surging noise in his head pushing him forward, the same thing that made his hands pick at themselves with happy agitation, the same thing that made him good at his job and fun at the pub and able to sleep with women. And at others he could feel that same pulse too physically, too materially, like it was going to start emerging through his skin.

I'll take a holiday after this, he thought, in the room in Hotel Gargano, and then to test it out he said the words aloud, imagining saying them to Edward, but he was unable to picture it, and realised he didn't know if 'after this' meant after Lucy was arrested, or after she was brought to trial, or after she was convicted, and then knew that there was no after this, this was it.

Absurdly, he wanted to cry. The pulsing mania helped him forget how small and alone he was almost all of the time but this story was a new level, and the enormity of what he was doing slipped through his usual defences. It was too much for him to be responsible for. The story was too big and upsetting and difficult, and he was only himself. He needed someone to look after him for a bit. He needed a girlfriend, maybe, or at the least a bit of mothering. If not a holiday then he would certainly make it home for a weekend soon. Shortly. In the meantime he did not have time for such feelings, and thought of Edward and his relentlessness. He gathered all the reserves he had of ambition and curiosity and incision and reminded himself he was unusual to be so plentifully gifted with these things, closed his eyes and visualised them welded together in a burning golden ball of energy that would sit in his centre and help him through the next few days, and began sketching out stories, stories which were not yet real but could become so, imagining what the family might give away over the next day and night.

3.

A knock jolted Richie into the physical agony of panic his mind had been trying to protect him from. He noticed a few years back that of the hours you would describe as sleep, those hours he was in bed with eyes closed, several of them were no longer really unconscious. The final hour or two before he actually left bed were spent in a suspended state through which the aware part of himself urged the still-asleep part not to wake. The aware part was guardian, feeling no anxiety itself but knowing that when it was met by the absented full consciousness then it would all come crashing down. The aware part soothed the other when it began reaching toward cognition, assured that it was fine to stay in the sleeping state a while longer, where nothing could hurt it.

You're okay, you're okay, you're okay, said the aware part. Sometimes it repeated Richie's personal self-soothing mantra, an affirmation he had once seen written out for a bold boy in his class at school who had terrible weeping explosions and as a result no friends. A teacher had written on a sticker for him and fixed it to his homework diary, for him to look at and repeat when he was upset: I'm a good person and other people think so too. And Richie's aware part said this to the other part to calm it down while it struggled toward the new day.

Today, though, there had not been a lengthy transition period, the knock coming just after eight o'clock, and the shock of this new day was far worse than the usual badness of those at home. His mind strained to make sense of his big white bed and the quality of sunlight coming through the window and then, once it had caught up, rejected the ostensible pleasantness of these things as the signals of terror they were. He recalled dimly hissing at his sister and father in the bar downstairs but there were large holes in his memory on either side of that scene. He tried to think if he had spoken any more, praying he had not invited the journalist into his room.

Clambering out of bed, he paused a moment and pressed with expertly calculated pressure on the tender right side of his lower torso which pained him as it did most mornings. Outside the door, a bag had been discreetly left, with a note on top reading 'I'll let you have something to eat and meet you back here in a while for the hair of the dog – Tom.' The bag contained three new pairs of boxers and socks, a blue cotton shirt, three plain t-shirts, and a pair of strange elasticated slacks suitable for an eighty-year-old to garden in, all from Marks & Spencer. He wondered if his father had received an identical package, and if not, how the person tasked with choosing the items had made their decisions.

He would wear his black jeans as usual, the same pair he had had for ten years, the weight gain since then all localised above where they sat on his body. He also had with him an old dark green knitted jumper that had belonged to Rose, inherited from her father, a huge ratty garment full of moth holes he had assimilated into the incoherent punk-adjacent aesthetic of his early twenties. He had dressed that way when his life had frozen in its place without him being aware that it was happening, so that he still dressed, now, at thirty-two, like he had been waylaid en route to a gig in a filthy basement.

There were some days he woke up and tried not to drink, and contrary to people's beliefs there were even some days when he did not drink. They were rare now but there were a few a month. Sometimes because an ailment was alarming him, sometimes because he was awash with depression and shame and couldn't bear the idea of leaving the flat to get more. Sometimes because he hadn't the money, very occasionally because he convinced himself he might try to give up again.

There was a time in his drinking when he went day on, day off. It meant that during the On Days he would drink enough to make sure he would feel too sick to want it the next day, and this meant he was only drinking four nights a week, which wasn't much more than a lot of people his age at the time. It seemed like a sufficient negotiation to make with the world, one of many he tried to strike with his drinking.

That system lasted a while, until he had been in London a year and it became clear that the fresh start had been no such thing and none of his attempts to make a life for himself had been, or were going to be, successful. The need for the days off stopped seeming so apparent when he hadn't shifts to work or interviews to do or evening classes to sample.

So now he would just drink a normal amount, every day, but not to that extreme degree he had before, and this was true until it wasn't, until one day he was drinking with the purposeful excess of the old On Days and every day was now an On Day. There were some days he woke up and tried not to drink, still – but this day, waking in the alien hotel room light, was not one of them.

He pulled on one of the clean t-shirts and the green jumper over it and the hotel robe over that for the hell of it, and took from the fridge a miniature vodka and a small bottle of orange juice, and poured them together into a heavy-bottomed glass on the bedside table.

4.

Trying not to show it, trying to keep her chin up, lessons in defensive dignity she had learned during her late pregnancy, Carmel was frightened and confused in the police station. She had tried to ask questions of the one who drove her in but he tutted and told her he didn't know anything and that someone or other was going to speak with her when they arrived. There was little more clarity when she arrived, hustled into a room by a team of officers who all blurred into one conciliatory, useless responder.

Is she under arrest? Carmel asked.

No, they replied, she was being held pending investigation.

How long can you keep her? she asked.

Usually it's only twenty-four hours, they said, but in the case of a serious crime like this one we have the power to extend it. We don't anticipate we will need to, but the investigation is ongoing as of today.

Can't she come home while you're investigating? she asked.

No. They hoped not to keep her longer than necessary. They were looking at the possibility of emergency local authority housing, akin to a special sort of foster home. They recognised it was not ideal but in such unusual circumstances sometimes it was the best option. Lucy could not return home for a variety of reasons, including that the home address was also the address of the victim's family. And I believe, said one of them carefully, you've got an arrangement with a paper to put you up in a hotel? So you aren't at your home either, are you?

She was taken aback by this, had inferred from the officer yesterday dropping her off to Hotel Gargano that it was all above board, that it may even have been something like a dual enterprise between the paper and the police. She noticed that officer wasn't here now, wondered if he had broken some rule. She reddened, seeing what this other one seemed to think of her, that she was swanning around like a great woman raking it in while her child was in jail. And she thought then of Richie and the bill he would run up if left unfettered, and that there was no reason a newspaper would pay for all of that and give them money in envelopes unless they thought they would print something to make it worthwhile.

That was only logical, she had known it all along, but last night it hadn't yet bothered her, when the impossibility of Lucy's guilt seemed blindingly obvious. Let them take the gamble, she had nothing to lose. That's how it had felt.

Really, who would care about a family like theirs? Theirs were ordinary human failings, tragedies too routine to be of note.

In the light of day in the station, things appeared different. They must really think Lucy had done it if they would keep such a small child in custody. She felt an aggressive momentum amongst the officers, moving toward a conclusion they seemed confident of and hungry for. Even if they weren't sure, perhaps they would be under enough pressure that they would press charges anyway. Now her mind was fragmenting, diffuse with competing urgencies, for she needed to get back to the hotel to make sure her family were not doing anything stupid, but before she could do that she needed also to see her daughter. She felt frightened again at this prospect, sitting in the corridor waiting to be led in. It wasn't fright connected to the police station, or to the situation. It wasn't even because she genuinely feared Lucy may have been responsible for the things they said she was, which she had not yet begun to do.

It was in fact the same fear she always had felt, since the day she gave birth, any time she was made to truly and fully turn her attention to Lucy. Lucy as a person, as a real human being, rather than a set of logistics or an abstracted concept.

Those times were few, on balance, much fewer than one might guess at in the life of a ten-year-old child. Rose had been there for eight of them, a constant but unobtrusive presence. There were the early years when Rose had all but assumed complete responsibiltity for mothering Lucy after it had become clear that Carmel had formed no attachment to her child. She in fact would go to lengths to strain away from her, walking for hours around the neighbourhood when she was still sore from the birth. Attempts were made by Rose and a health visitor to encourage her, but she receded further. The cunning of her mind became apparent again; the grotesque, seemingly limitless ability to separate out and repress certain parts of reality.

When the baby screamed she was able to sit in the same room and not react at all. Sometimes after a long while she would leave and sit on the porch still in her nightdress, picking her cuticles and looking down into the courtyard below at the children playing, whose lives seemed more tolerable and visible than that of the baby actually belonging to her. When gently steered and then eventually remonstrated with for her lack of caring she appeared to absorb the instruction, would smile vaguely and agree, but nothing changed.

Rose reached toward the child naturally and without resentment. Her utility, her necessity, helped calm the otherwise unbearable discomfort of how rapidly and severely her family had been damaged – a family which had seemed not long ago one of only average unhappiness.

Once in school, Lucy could be thought of mostly as an entity comprising schedules, and tasks to be dealt with. There was only a ninety-minute interlude between the time when Carmel would pick her up and feed her a snack, forcefully tuning out her chatter and questions, and the time when Rose came home from work. Then Carmel often left for the evening shift at the late-night convenience shop which was situated in a tucked-away-enough street that there were only a few drunks an hour calling in to top up, and she read for the rest of the time, library books or magazines from the shop. She browsed quickly through the ones for older women, their alien worlds of dating and homemaking, finding the letters pages in the likes of *Just Seventeen* most compelling. One girl wrote in to say

Recently, I was at a party and met a boy I thought was really nice. We both got drunk and ended up having sex without contraception. I wouldn't have done it if I'd been sober, and afterwards I felt so cheap and dirty. I was a virgin before this happened and I'd always hoped that when I lost my virginity it would be with someone I cared for, and it would be a loving and pleasurable experience. It didn't turn out that way. When my period was late, I became so worried, thinking I must be pregnant. Eventually, my period arrived and the relief I felt has led me to write this letter. I feel I nearly ruined my life because I got drunk, and I'm never going to let this happen again. I've learned my lesson the hard way, and hope you print this to help other people realise how stupid it is to behave like this. Kelly.

Bully for you, you smug bitch, thought Carmel – what hard way?

In *19 Magazine* another was published which read:

My mother and I are in a row because she objects to my boyfriend. He is a few years older and already working, while I am still in school and hoping to go to university. She tells me she is afraid that I will get carried away and lose control and could end up pregnant, but the thing is, I am already having sex with him. We do use condoms and are careful. Should I tell my mum this and try to be honest with her and reassure her we are being responsible? Or is that running a risk she will totally stop me seeing him at all? Please write back as I can't stand fighting with my mum but I do love my boyfriend.

Carmel found herself tearing up, closing her eyes to stop them spilling. She allowed herself the rare torture of imagining that things had been different for her, imagining she had told Rose about Derek, imagining she had been forced to stop before he decided to leave her and before there was a baby, keeping not just her life but her pride.

Carmel wasn't cruel to the child. She never hit or hurt her. Her words were brisk and few rather than cutting. She had simply arranged things so that she need never sit down and confront the still insane reality of her existence, this thing that was made of her and Derek. Rose had made that easy, her love for both of them enabling it all. She even felt guilty for dying, in the end. She said so to Carmel. She was sorry she couldn't help her for longer. This opened inside Carmel an unprecedented torrent of self-loathing and recrimination which needed to be immediately suppressed for survival. She thought bitterly of her relationship with Rose in the life before, how effortlessly intimate it had been. And how, now, as she died, everything was poisoned with quantities of obligation which could never be apologised for adequately and so could never be voiced at all.

A part of her knew that all she really had to do to allow Rose to die in peace was assure her that she was ready now to love and protect Lucy, that she had been prepared so well for the task by Rose that it was going to come easily in her absence. But she could think of no way in which to say these things convincingly, and instead spoke to her during the final weeks only of things from the past.

Do you remember that Saturday when I was helping you clean up at the nuns' houses by the school and we stopped to sit in the grass in the sun, and one of them came out to us and told us to leave? And I was so embarrassed and you said not to mind her. And do you remember after a few steps there was a gust of wind and a ten-pound note blew out of the bushes and landed right at your feet like magic and you picked it straight up and put it in your pocket without even checking if the nun was watching, and we went into town to Greer's and had two cakes each sitting outside and watching everyone go by, and you said not to tell the lads or they would be jealous?

And do you remember when I found out Santa wasn't real because I walked in on Daddy getting changed into the costume and screamed and woke you up?

And do you remember when we were at the beach that time and Richie stepped on a bee and it stung him and he wouldn't stop crying, but it turned out he was crying because he felt bad for the bee dying?

These were rhetorical questions. Carmel knew that Rose had not forgotten. She remembered everything, right to the end.

5.

Carmel saw Lucy alone for only a few minutes. She took her in, the spindly body colouring in a book, this small dark creature that was so like herself.

She tried to imagine how a body like that could have the power and will to hurt another, to kill.

She could not move the parts correctly in her mind for it to cohere, when she thought of how the arms would have to work they dislocated and floated away, the picture would not be made.

In this way she still believed in the impossibility of her daughter's guilt, but there was a new bloom of dread and doubt too. It came from seeing, awed, that Lucy seemed content and satisfied sitting in this room. This prospect hadn't entered her mind. She expected that she would have to calm her hysteria, prise the clawing hands away when she left. What could such unnatural calmness mean?

She wanted to ask her. Of course she did.

She tried to form the words, which all sounded hideously inadequate.

Did you hurt the baby? she kept trying to say, but that felt soft, a cloying cover-up for the monstrosity she was trying to ask after.

She realised with a spark of quick shame that she did not have an intuitive sense of what level of cognition Lucy was operating under when it came to such matters. Could she speak to her in a direct manner, or would such bluntness be incomprehensible? Was she still cosseted in the vagueness of early childhood, or was she more like an adolescent? Did she believe in God? In heaven and hell?

Rose's death had created another condition in which it was possible and even reasonable to ignore Lucy's life. The grief was so bitter and consuming that it left no space to consider anything else, an extended version of the way in which a terrible hangover gives you permission to ignore the day's responsibilities, because they have become functionally impossible. The unfairness of the loss was total and occupying, its aggressive suddenness – she had been diagnosed with cancer and died of it in the space of eight weeks. That Carmel kept going to work, that the child went to school most days and ate enough, felt like an inordinate performance of capability.

She had never, she thought now, really spoken to Lucy about what happened to Rose, what death was at all. Rose had simply left the flat one day and never returned. She remembered now that when arrangements were being discussed for the funeral, Lucy had asked if Rose would be able to breathe inside the coffin, and that Carmel and her father had met eyes and not responded.

The words caught in her dry throat and did not emerge. Even through the panic, sitting there forced to look at this child, her child who was a stranger to her, she knew also the absurdity of the situation. She was mute in this most crucial moment, this moment in which it was the most imperative to take action, because of a feeling akin to social anxiety. She was stumbling over the most important question she would ever ask because she felt awkward. As if something as ridiculous as this could stop her, as if such frivolous character deficits as these were going to leave them submerged in silence. And yet they did, and she only sat with her daughter watching her draw, telling her once that it wouldn't be long until she came home, briefly reaching out to touch her wrist, and then withdrawing.

6.

John took in the bag of clothing and after inspecting the contents threw it to the side of the bed, staying in his own undershirt and trousers. He saw from the note that he wasn't to be summoned until the evening for an audience with the newspaper man. He looked out at the fine weather. Though he knew he couldn't leave, he thought he might go and sit in the gardens for a while in the afternoon. Until then he would remain in the room and watch television and order up breakfast. The whole day rolled out before him, imbued with the dignity and solemn pleasure of a man's last one.

Like his granddaughter eight miles away he felt relief that things had broken down so irrefutably. Finally something had happened to halt the way he staggered on through life in contravention of the truth inside himself. This perverse ongoingness was especially obscene since Rose died, but really it had been the case since Carmel got pregnant and they moved, but really it had been before that when his first wife left him, but really it had been when his father died, but really it had been his whole life.

Ordinarily his insistent solitude was surrounded by the presence of his family, making it aggressive, but he didn't necessarily want this. He didn't think of himself as a cruel

109

man. He only wanted to be alone, and he savoured this last day as one in which his aloneness would be harmless and appropriate.

Today, he would drink. He would drink with purpose and discernment.

He had always drank often, and eventually daily, but it was with a different spirit to the one his son drank with.

He envied Richie it at times, the wildness of his thirst, at least until the demands of the thirst mandated the repetitive misery he now lived within. But before that, when the moments of truly ugly excess could still be seen as innocent outliers, the way Richie drank looked attractive to his father. Richie loved what he drank and came alive with it, was bestowed with great reserves of life and energy. He shed the usual nervy, downtrodden aura, the avoidance of eye contact, and seemed free and open, musical and eloquent. For John, drinking had never been that way. It was only a kind of busy work and maintenance. It was something to do with your hands and your body which could be counted on. He only ever drank cheaply and quickly for this reason.

Today, though, today he would choose carefully, enjoy at his leisure and wait for the rest to unfold. On the television a rerun of a drama called *Who Bombed Birmingham?* played, which he watched with detached interest while he opened the first bottle of wine, to see if he liked wine after all.

7.

At midday Tom returned to Richie's room and was pleased to see he had already begun drinking. He looked lively enough, well even, sitting at the bureau by the window flicking through a Bible with the television on at half volume in the background. Tom had brought things to make Bloody Marys and set them down on the table.

What's this? he asked, inclining his head to the Bible. Checking to see if you've been naughty or nice?

It was a minor risk. He wanted to approach Richie in the spirit of peers, lads together, but didn't know what his levels of sensitivity were.

He smiled back in a moment of surprise and genuine mirth and Tom saw that he had once been handsome. He looked nothing like Carmel, who must have inherited her darkness from the dead mother. His colouring was sandy and reddish, bad luck for a drinker, and he had a similar delicate nose to his father's. Clear blue eyes not yet obscured with yellow or burst blood vessels as they one day would be. And though it was shrouded in a layer of puffiness the structure of his face was fine too, pronounced cheekbones and a strong chin.

Tom's heart performed the familiar bend of attraction and worry it always did when he saw a good-looking man who was past his prime, the urge to kiss him and bring him back to life. Because men were familiar there was something in his attractions to them which was also self-conciliatory. He felt the urge to use his affection to comfort them about things he himself was concerned by.

I haven't looked at one since school, said Richie, shutting the Bible over, thought I should check to see if there have been any major updates – he raised his glass in salute before draining it – the drunk shall inherit the earth, something like that.

Amen. Can I make you one of these? asked Tom, waving the litre of tomato juice and Tabasco.

First time for everything, Richie consented, and moved over to sit at the table with him.

Really, you've never had one of these?

Not a common sight in Waterford, and I wasn't training up on any new enterprises once I got over here. More sticking with the classics, you know yourself. Tried and true.

111

I'm addicted to them, Tom said in a confidential tone of voice, instantly regretting his casual hyperbole. There's nothing better for a hangover. Gets you drunk again but the spice gives you a shock to the system as well.

Hah – a bit like a speedball then.

A speedball?

Heroin and cocaine, the high and the low counteracting each other. Or working together I suppose. Killed John Belushi if I remember correctly.

Tom wondered if he should unspool that thread. He hadn't heard anything to suggest there were drugs at play but it wouldn't be surprising, could make for a whole other element to the coverage. He mentally shelved it for later, wanting to continue the relaxed dynamic for a while.

On the television John Hurt was a journalist investigating the Birmingham pub bombings, and both men idly watched for a few moments.

It's probably good you weren't here for all that, Tom remarked. Must have been even worse than it is now.

Richie smiled without looking at him.

It's possible, he said. You know, when we moved over here first and I did a few shifts in a pub on the Rye, there was a regular who hated my fucking guts, kept telling me he had a friend who was shot in Derry. I've never been to Derry in my life. Anyway, he never stopped, he couldn't get over it. Gave him something to do, probably. I didn't take much notice, but the thing I always remember is him turning to me one day and asking, was I an altar boy? I said I was, only briefly, but I was. And he said I must have been touching up children the whole time. I wanted to say to him, you've got your facts wrong, buddy. It would have been me getting touched up, not the other way round.

He laughed, shaking his head with some fondness or nostalgia.

What was it like then, when you all moved here? asked Tom.

Well it was brilliant really, for a while. In a way. For me, I mean, and only for a short while. Do you know how rare it is to start over?

He stopped, as though he wanted Tom to actually answer, but he couldn't. Leaving his girlfriends, moving to London, starting at the paper – these were organic progressions, not second chances.

See? So rare you've never done it, though I'm sure you will at some stage. Man like you with lots of resources and a job where you make a lot of enemies. I can see you throwing it all in one day and moving to Mexico or hopping on a yacht. I used to dream about starting over, long before we came to London. I dreamed about it since before there was even anything wrong with my life. I used to watch *Dynasty* with Rose sometimes and have these fantasies I'd go asleep and wake up in America. It wasn't the being rich – I even felt it when we watched *Little House on the Prairie*, for Christ's sake! I just had this incredible urge to start from the start and wipe out anything I had done or who I was, to even be from a different country, and that's what it felt like at first when I moved over here.

You were happy, all of you? Tom asked.

No, no, said Richie, animated and dismissive, I'm not talking about them. For once I'm not talking about any of them. I was happy. Me. I knew things were difficult and sad, what had happened to Carmel, but I was happy at first. It was out of nowhere and I didn't really have a choice, the way I'd dreamt about it just happening beyond my control when I was younger. I had to come over with them because they were going to rent out the house and I'd have nowhere to stay.

I thought – this will make you laugh – I thought I'd live in that flat with them for a few weeks while I found a job and then I'd move into Camden and buy my own flat. Buy, mind you, not rent. I don't know what job I thought I'd get with a Leaving Certificate and six weeks' experience in a Waterford cafe, but there's always some bit of you that still believes the 'streets are paved with gold' horse shite, no matter how many broke winos come home or, worse, die here too ashamed to go home. Which I expect is exactly what I'll do. Although, who knows? With all this – he gestured at Tom – it might be more peaceful to go home and die in Waterford.

Why are you talking about dying, Richie? asked Tom softly. You're a young man.

How young would you say I am? If you didn't know. He met Tom's eyes, still smiling and with a gleam of fear and dark amusement in his own. How old would you say, eh? I know what I look like. I know what I am. Just because I don't bring it up all the time, doesn't mean I don't see it. I've tried it that way as well actually – making a joke of it, while I'm having a drink. People don't like that too much. They don't mind drinking with you if you pretend it's all normal and fine and the same as having a pint with any old pal, but if you point out, even with a light heart, that they are having a companionable drink with a full-time drunk, they don't like that! Oh, no! And that's a shame because I'll tell you something Tom: I really like drinking with people. I love drinking with people. That's why I'm a drunk. Ironically, because now I'm a drunk I've scared everyone off. But that's why, because I love people. I'll tell you how bad I'm getting, after I got your note this morning I sat here feeling delighted with myself, couldn't wait until you came back, I'm that fucking lonely. Just because you're a pleasant person who seems to have a brain and I knew you would drink with me. Now how sick is that? Getting excited to have a drink with you, in the middle of everything that's going on.

I think it's perfectly normal you would rather not be alone, said Tom using his powerful assurance voice.

I'd rather I was never alone, that's the God's honest truth. I've been afraid to be alone since the day I was born, and it's all I ever am. You might think the opposite, that we're all on top of each other in that little flat, but I am always, always alone. Imagine there was something you couldn't stand for even a day, and you have to stand it every day, for your whole life?

He was working himself up now and Tom was aware that he was going to cry.

Oh God, oh God, he was choking out the words as though they disgusted him, oh God, don't let me die on my own, and looked at Tom desperately as he said it, as though he were God, as though he could prevent it.

Part V

RICHIE
Waterford, 1979

1.

While Carmel was falling in love with Derek O'Toole, Richie was twenty-one and ready to begin his life. Somehow three years had passed since he had left school and to his surprise nobody had made him do anything since the day he walked out of his final exam. He hadn't made a plan because he wanted to take the summer off to have a good time. When the summer ended he felt no more inclination to do anything than he had before it, so he allowed himself another year to decide on the next move.

In the interim he signed on to the dole and worked cash-in-hand in a few pubs around town when they needed someone for busy periods, and rented a box room in Ballybeg on an informal basis from the older brother of a girl he was seeing. After the girl broke up with him the brother threw him out, sick of his prodigious vomiting and foul-smelling 3 a.m. meals left hardening on the counter, leaving the single box of possessions on the front door step. Following this inconvenience he took the same approach to accommodation as he took to working, taking it up whenever it surfaced but not seeking it with any urgency. In between situations there was always Mayor's Walk, which was tolerable so long as he used it only for sleep and stayed out of his father's way as much as possible.

He didn't know why he had expected an intervention, except that it seemed most everyone else he went to school with had one. Either they had made up their minds to study or train or become an apprentice or their parents had proposed a certain kind of job, in some cases even arranged the interview for them. A few moved far away which was a definitive enough action on its own without also needing a career. The ones who couldn't find anything and went on the dole like him were making plans to try Dublin and London.

It was so tense in Mayor's Walk in the final few years of school that all his focus was on the day he could leave and not be under anyone's control any more, he had never seen beyond that. Nor had anyone broached the subject with him. After a substantial amount of time had passed, Rose would occasionally ask if he had any plans when he called in to the house. She always asked while making the tea or cooking, said it casually as though it was nothing to her either way.

The casualness was not unpleasant, or intended to convey indifference, but because of a natural gulf – an awkward absence of natural authority – that existed between she and Richie because they were not related by blood. This gulf varied in its depth over the years, sometimes feeling hardly present at all, but as he had reached his late teenage years it had shifted into a permanent state of significance, separating the two of them. This estrangement was prodded at and worsened by his father, who would call attention to it at any opportunity. If Rose gave some passing bit of advice, John would reflexively say, What would you know, you're not his mother, and both Rose and Richie would be embarrassed into silence.

So Rose had not guided him as she surely would

Carmel when she graduated. And his father had never brought the subject up except to remind him that when school ended he would be expected to pay rent if he stayed in the house.

His father had, to be fair, assumed a general, blanket stance of apathy toward employment as a concept, ever since he had been forcibly removed from the workforce by a catastrophic injury suffered in the factory before Richie was born. One arm had been crushed to near uselessness, and a network of damaged nerves caused him tolerable but constant discomfort. Perhaps it was because of this he could not bring himself to feign enthusiasm for Richie beginning his years as an employable man. Perhaps he liked to know that his son was of as little material value as he felt himself to be.

The year elapsed and still nothing happened to suggest a course of action. He was surprised that no event had occurred to shape the future, but not unduly alarmed.

He had always drank with the resourceful enthusiasm of someone afraid it would be taken away at any moment, and he began to realise that was exactly what he had expected to happen – that a plan or circumstance would announce itself in his life to make the way he drank impossible.

He felt a sense of indignation when he began to notice slight physical signs of his abuse – around his nostrils threaded veins were becoming apparent, and the skin around his eyelids was often swollen and a livid corpse-like purple.

How was this possible, when he was only twenty?

His stomach, too, was suffering inordinately for what seemed to him only usual behaviour. He shifted restlessly in his bed, the feeling of trapped air migrating around his guts and sometimes suddenly changing tack so that it felt as though it had settled dangerously in his chest.

He wondered could you have a heart attack from

constipation and diarrhoea, the tension creeping over his heart and around the back of his shoulders, a jagged and precarious net of pain which worsened with every breath he took, so that he could only take small shallow ones which did not move his body at all and he felt that he might lose consciousness.

It did sound worrying, he knew that, but he struggled to feel worried. He was with people every night of the week who drank the same way he did, what made him so different that he was going to die of it? When there was nobody obvious to hand, he walked down to the new clubhouse the bikers had started in a shed off Paddy Brown's Road, calling themselves the Freewheelers. Of course he did not think yet about the fact that the rota of people alternated through his own evenings which remained the same, their once-a-week sprees fitting in seamlessly to his full-time pursuit.

But still. Not to worry. Something would make itself known, he assumed, and he would make the most of the leisure now, seeing his friends as much as he liked, long hilarious nights around kitchen tables, the burst of euphoria that came with true, painful laughter was so extreme and powerful that it felt obviously to be the real point of life.

One afternoon in town when he was walking around with a bottle of Lucozade waiting for one of the lads to finish work and meet him, he passed a little store front being renovated in the Apple Market and asked the fellow painting the sign what was coming in.

An Italian restaurant, he said looking pleased. The man who bought it is moving down from Dublin, but he's from Rome originally he told me.

Richie felt a rare stir of decisiveness and desire and asked if he knew were they looking for staff.

I'd say they must be, come back on Saturday when I'm finishing up and I'll write down his phone number for you.

He thanked the fellow and walked on feeling warm,

wonderful, the glow of volition inside him and rendering the evening ahead rich and meaningful.

2.

Richie had his first shift at Mario's three weeks later, the day before the grand opening.

Who's Mario? he asked Bella, the daughter of the owner who was explaining the menu and feeding the new staff little samples in dinky paper cups then demanding they give her three adjectives to describe what they tasted.

Mario is nobody, she sighed, My father thought people would like that name better than any of ours. He's been called Phil his whole life, which doesn't exactly sing with Italian glamour.

Why not Bella's? Richie asked her, this harried, pretty woman in her thirties not wearing a ring.

She laughed. Let's just say I wasn't the favoured child until very recently, when I was the only one who would move down here to do this, she gestured around at the dangling fairy lights and fake plants they had just festooned the low ceiling with.

Do your brothers and sisters not have any interest in restaurants?

No. My sister is married and has young children to look after and my brothers are interested in having a lot of money and people knowing who they are. Maybe they would have wanted it if it was in Dublin or London or Rome but not down here, she said, and he felt mildly cut.

He didn't like when people spoke about Waterford as though it wasn't a real place. It made his lack of momentum feel darker than it usually did. She noticed him turn away and end his curiosity and touched him lightly on his shoulder.

I don't mean to offend you. I like it just fine here. I think it suits me, and he smiled back at her, wanting to make her like it even more than she did, wanting for things to be a success and her to become the golden child of the family.

The waiters were all given white shirts and waistcoats and green aprons to wear because that was the usual get-up in Italy and he felt pleasure trying it on that evening. He had a room let for eight weeks in Merchant's Quay and he thought after that he would have enough wages saved to find somewhere more settled, longer-term.

The menu was deliberately crowd-pleasing, almost everyone ordered pizzas and spaghetti bolognese and lasagne, but there was a slightly more challenging special every day which Richie enjoyed hearing about from Bella and tasting. He repeated with fondness her enthusiastic advocation for each one even to families who expressed their forceful disinterest toward him as he spoke, the ravioli filled with squash puree and walnut sauce, the squid and roasted red peppers, the gnocchi made with spinach and goat's cheese.

Bella had a friend of hers come and help her paint a big mural on one wall of a bountiful table full of food and wine, surrounded by laughing friends touching glasses. Bella wasn't as good a painter as her friend but Richie could see it was meaningful to her to be a part of it, and he enjoyed seeing the small sliver of tongue poking out of her mouth while she concentrated.

After the first week, having survived his first minor disasters, he began to feel that he was good at what he was doing and that it made sense of him as a person somehow. Bella appreciated him. One evening she came into the kitchen white-faced and said she had accidentally served meat to a man who claimed he was a lifelong vegetarian who had never endured the passing of flesh over his lips before.

Which one? asked Richie, immediately suspicious. She described him, Kevin, a pretentious and pretty boy Richie had gone to school with whose current passion was cultivating an air of long-haired mysticism. He scoffed. Tell him I saw him with his face in a bag of sausage and chips every Saturday night for five years, he told her.

She didn't, but the knowledge made her laugh, and calmed her down.

He was at ease moving around, fluid and intuitive. It was because it felt like a performance, he thought. Every night was like the beginning of a new play in which he held a peripheral but crucial role. There was something extremely soothing in the way he was simultaneously on show and necessarily discreet. It was a situation which addressed the discomfort of his life to this point, the dread of ever being a burden on others and the dread of nobody ever paying attention to him. His fear of other people receded in this specificity, where he had a role to fulfil and information to impart and receive and because he was playing a role he was able to respect himself more than he did at other times, straightening his back and making eye contact and smiling boldly.

3.

Six weeks in, on a Friday evening after service ended he drank three large glasses of leftover wine with Bella and Luke, the nicest chef. He was a gregarious Frenchman who made up for being from the wrong romantic European country with the extravagant smacking sounds of enjoyment he made as he cooked, and a general enthusiasm for bringing new food to this place he had moved to for love and where he had been routinely appalled ever since by the sullenly ugly, limp meals on offer. The three of them gossiped about the other two waiting staff, Deirdre and Thomas, teenagers whom they suspected of recently beginning an affair.

Deirdre is always smiling now, have you noticed that? asked Bella, and it's ever since we had the night out and the two of them went off together at the end of it.

Maybe she's just smiling because she loves pasta so much, said Richie, and they laughed and he was pleased.

You love pasta so much, said Luke fondly, reaching over and pinching his cheek, you're getting nice and fat now.

Hey! said Richie, but he had always enjoyed being teased with obvious affection and he didn't mind it at all.

No, man, it's a good thing, said Luke. You looked bad when you first started. Not joking, I asked her if she was sure you were going to keep turning up. But you're doing so great. My best waiter, no mistakes.

Bella smiled at the two of them dopily, her low tolerance for alcohol sated by her share of the now-empty bottle.

I'm tired. Can you open up in the morning, Rich? Remember we have a birthday lunch booking at midday so get here by half-nine to set up, please. I'll be here at eleven, and she slid the second set of keys over to him.

When Richie left it was only a little after midnight, and he was exultant in the fine weather and the warmth of his new friendships. He walked down onto the quay and felt his body to be stronger and more useful than before, and a dreamy liquidity beginning in his limbs from what he had drank. It was so lovely to be able to drink only a little bit, he thought. Working at the restaurant had been good for him in that way. He was busy trying to get it right and be present for Bella and the rest of them and hadn't seen much of his usual crowd, hadn't drank in that way for a few weeks now. This didn't feel like a sacrifice because he had a drink with the restaurant staff most nights.

These evenings tended to end with one or more of them

yawning compellingly, reminding the rest that they were gathered together because they had worked hard for a long time and that they would do so again tomorrow. There was drunkenness, but not the sort which caused physical intrusions the like of which had troubled him before he started to work there. All of this he reflected upon on his languid stroll, glad and surprised that something so significant could change without any enormous will or effort on his part. He had been right, perhaps, that it hadn't been himself but only his circumstances which needed shifting. He was so pleased, in fact, so proud of the departure from his old way of being, that it occurred to him he could go and see the usual crowd right that moment, and have some more to drink with them.

He was, as it happened, passing the building where his friend Gary Clancy lived and had hosted drinking sessions every Friday night for the past year, and he stopped and stood outside of the door. He thought for a moment, doing a quick calculation and figured if he got to sleep by three he would be absolutely fine to get to the restaurant for half-nine. Young man, full of health, life, light. He could do anything, do it all.

He was buzzed upstairs and received with a rousing round of whooping and shouts of Here he is, the man himself!, a welcome phrase which had always struck Richie as almost unbearably cheering, that feeling of everyone being happy to see you, telling you the night had been lacking something before your arrival. Sitting around the kitchen table were Clancy and four other fellows he knew to varying degrees, boys he had been to school with, and one older man whom he knew only to see. The man was exotically named Lucien though he was a lifelong local and suspected of giving himself the title. He was also, Richie recalled vaguely, suspected of being gay because he lived alone with two cats and put care into his appearance. This suspicion was overlooked or forgiven though because the appearance

127

he took care with was one of great ferocity, safety pins stuck into all manner of surfaces, and hair spiked into enormous threatening towers. In Camden maybe Lucien would have been nothing remarkable but here the dedication to an image as singular and unusual as this was regarded with a twisted respect. To stand out was so abhorrent and insane that someone who did it fully on purpose was accepted as a mad genius. Richie, who had always despaired of his every variance, could see that it almost didn't matter what you were – so long as you swore yourself to it with total arrogant pride there was little anyone could do to use it against you.

Two yellow-blonde girls he didn't know sat on an armchair, spilling limbs over each other and whispering privately, almost primly despite the bottles of sticky cider they were huddled round and the fags with dangling long ash in their hands, occasionally hooting with laughter. One of them looked up at him when he scraped out a chair to join the table, he nodded hello and in response she crossed her eyes very quickly and fully before returning to her conversation, which made him smile. He apologised for not having brought anything to drink.

Not at all, Richie boy, admonished Clancy, and drew out a new bottle of vodka and a two-litre of red lemonade, You probably left this here another time, anyway. Drink up. Where have you been the last while, we missed you.

He enjoyed hearing this, of course he did. He told them about the new job and that he'd been busy settling in, but he'd missed them too. He said this bashfully, but he liked that they were saying these things to each other, it made his being there alright. These were his friends. He tipped his cup toward the other lads and said, Nice to meet you, to Lucien, who winked his approval back as Richie downed his drink in one. They all cheered and a spark of celebration entered the room. Mark – a nice introspective guy who had been derisively nicknamed Dark Mark in school because of his thoughtfulness which sometimes appeared to be moodiness but really wasn't, not in any bad way – Mark was having a baby with the girl he'd been with since third year in school. He had just found out a week before. They cheersed to that again, and Clancy asked him, How does that feel, are you shitting it?

Gary, said one of the girls sharply, so that Richie assumed she was Gary's girlfriend and did not appreciate the implication that lifelong commitments were something to be avoided.

No, it's grand, said Mark. It is scary, like, yeah, but I think it will be good craic. I'm one of four and I always thought I'd want the same as that, none of us were ever alone for five minutes but in a nice way, you know, feeling part of the gang.

And Richie thought no, he did not know, couldn't imagine a feeling like that. He drank again, draining the second cup, feeling it burn into his chest cavity and the bubble of levity and pleasure travel further into his brain.

I'm proud of you Mark, I think you'll be a smashing dad, said Lucien quietly. He stood up and put on a record, something loud and indecipherable and modern-sounding, exciting.

I don't know, said Paul, one of the other lads from their year. Wasn't it Mark who rang Mr Hutchinson that time and told him his son was dead?

There was a moment of quiet while they sorted through the past to clarify the memory and once they had they began to laugh, really, really laugh, until it felt like coming up on drugs and there was no way to escape it. Oh, oh, they cried, wiping tears from their eyes and throwing their heads back, shaking themselves to try and recover.

They had been eleven and it was April Fool's Day. Their teacher Mr Hutchinson was a friend of one of their fathers, and it was decided for the prank that year they would get his phone number from the father's address book and call him. Mark was the calmest of them and one of the funniest, so he was chosen, and they pooled their coins at the phone box and dialled the number. It was only as Mr Hutchinson answered that Mark realised they hadn't actually planned for what to say if he answered, there was no script to follow. Desperately grasping in his mind for anything to fix on, he recalled that Mr Hutchinson had an adult son in Dublin.

Hello? Hello? said Mr Hutchinson.

Hello, sir, said Mark in a gruff disguise voice, and all the rest of them listening instantly dissolved into silent giggles, Mr Hutchinson?

Yes that's me.

Mr Hutchinson . . . Panic setting in now, needing to do something, make a big splash, impress everyone, Mr Hutchinson, I'm very sorry to tell you this but your son is dead. Up in Dublin. Your son died.

There was silence on the other end of the phone and surrounding him amongst the gawping faces of his friends. Then he heard a gasp down the line, and weak murmuring sound.

Oh, no, oh, Danny, no, no, please, no.

Mark's eyes widened and he said in his ordinary voice, No, no, don't worry Mr Hutchinson, it's only an April Fool, don't worry at all, please don't worry, and slammed the phone down.

He spun round to look at the others, begging them with his eyes to tell him it was going to be okay and he was alright. Richie had his hand over his mouth and was shaking his head side to side involuntarily, trying to go back in time. There was a general sense of appalled shock. Then Paul and another boy had let out a few shrill sniggers, and then the whole lot of them had collapsed with hysterical disbelieving laughter, even Richie. He remembered how it had come flying out of

130

him, out of the depths of his chest like a cough would, hacking and unstoppable. They laughed and laughed at the disgraceful absurdity of it, at how amazingly far Mark had overshot. They knew that it was a dreadful thing, and that they would soon pay for how bad it was, but for the moment they banged and thumped the phone box in their perverse glee, and it was a beautiful thing as well as an ugly one.

They laughed the same way now, ten years later and most of the same lads sitting around that kitchen table. When Richie met the eyes of another of them he started all over again. They reached out blindly for one another's arms to squeeze for emphasis, and the physical sensation of happiness was so immense that Richie could hardly believe he had almost not come here tonight.

4.

Near 4 a.m. there was an awareness that the drink would be gone before long, Clancy shaking the near-empty bottle as he poured from it.

We're almost out, boys and girls, he said with a sigh. The room was dense with smoke and good feeling. Richie, could you get a bottle of something from the restaurant do you think?

Richie, vibrantly red in the face already, flushed further and exhaled in a conciliatory way. Ahh, he said, Ahh, I don't think so. They take the stock all the time.

Clancy put his hand on his heart in a swooning gesture of offence. Of course they do, I'm not suggesting we rob the place, who do you take me for? We'll get it back to them later today, I'm good for it. It might not be too often we're all together like this, Mark about to reproduce and all.

It's only because of this uncivilised country, said Lucien languidly, reclining on the armchair with one of the sleeping

131

girls curled around his shoulders like an enormous drunk cat. When I was in Paris we went out to get bread when the bakeries opened at dawn and bought wine to drink while we queued for it. Only in Ireland do the government treat its people as too incompetent to decide what to do with their bodies.

Richie nodded forcefully despite thinking to himself that this was surely not a quite accurate summary of world politics.

All the same he had to admit that eating a lot of bread and drinking wine sounded an extremely appealing concept in this moment. Maybe there would be bread handy to take at Mario's as well as wine. The inside of his chest felt hollow and acrid and he wanted to push something soft down his oesophagus. He thought also of how good it would feel to have a whole bottle of cool white wine before him. Like vodka, white wine had a quality of bottomless enjoyment. Not only did he have infinite tolerance for consuming them, they also had the capacity to endlessly promise good cheer. So long as there was more of them there was more pleasure to be had. This promise was not exactly a false one. It was true that whatever way they interacted with his brain he could feel no worry or sadness so long as they kept him company. Enough beer made him full and grumpy and red wine made him fall asleep, there had never so far in his life been a time when he had tired willingly of drinking vodka or white wine, stopping only because he couldn't get any more.

Before long they had persuaded him that it wasn't such a big production as he was making it, and they would have the bottles replaced by the end of the day. He did notice that they were bottles plural now rather than singular but this was to be expected. One bottle between them would be gone in a few minutes, if he was going to go all the way there he may as well pick up a few. They were good for it, they weren't mean lads. For the most part they weren't short of a few quid. He was only doing this because they couldn't get it anywhere else.

I'll come with you, said Lucien, standing and stretching. I need the walk.

A brief absurd flare of alarm as Richie thought of the rumours of him being gay or otherwise odd, then he scolded himself for being judgemental. The streets were empty but strewn with recently abandoned junk food which made him feel a moment of worry as he understood that the things they were doing had ended for the rest of the city.

The night is young, said Lucien, catching his eye and wriggling his brows enigmatically. He was quite handsome beneath the ghostly make-up, a strong big nose and a mouth which stretched so wide it made Richie think of the tragedy and comedy theatre masks.

Is it still night? Richie asked, and began doing the latest and what would turn out to be final set of calculations: If we get back by five I'll stop drinking at seven and have a shower and then I'll be fine to get back in to open up. He had stopped kidding himself about sleep now.

Who cares? said Lucien, You decide. All of the things you believe are fixed are just a matter of words. Call them something different and they change. It's night if we want it to be, because whatever it is, it's our own to spend. My old man used to obsess over the hours between 8 and 10 p.m., none of us or even my mam were allowed to talk to him then because he said it was the only part of his life that belonged to him. For years I had that too, I believed there was something special and sacred about night-time. And then I grew up a bit, got to see a few things, and I realised it was all a con and a trick to keep people like him in their place. In reality it can be night-time whenever you like – those things we like about night-time, we can have them whenever we like if we just decide to have them. There's no special rule that says it has to be dark when you have a drink, or light when you start work. Good morning, goodnight, happy Christmas – who cares? Live how you want to, when you want to. That's the trick.

He had linked Richie's arm loosely as he spoke which made him feel nervous and luxurious with novelty. They arrived to the restaurant, Lucien singing Christmas songs beneath his breath, light irresistible mania. Richie opened the door and led them toward the storeroom where he picked up two bottles of white wine, feeling relieved by their slender familiar weight. Lucien was picking up more, turning something out of a bag and filling it with red wine.

I don't think we should take that much, Richie said, mildly.

Relax, kid. It's only because I don't drink white wine, said Lucien and shrugged at the perfect and irrefutable logic he had employed.

Richie would not in future remember a full narrative trajectory from this time onward, only moments and images and the feeling of time dipping in and out haphazardly. When he tried to recall the anxiety he must surely have felt, there was nothing, only smooth absence. For a while, later, this was the focus of his agony: that he couldn't recall feeling even slightly bothered about what would in a matter of hours fill him with a degree and quantity of shame which he had never withstood before. The mystery of his missing anxiety plagued him in the aftermath, as though there was some moment of transition he could identify if he looked long enough, between the unfeeling person and the feeling one which followed. How could it be, he thought frantically, how could it be that the same situation hours apart could affect him with such wild difference?

But it was true, and there was no mystery to solve. There was no key moment, no switch flipped. He was not repressing a memory of secret panic which he had hidden from Lucien. Lucien had not threatened him with violence, or even with dislike. It was only that the time had come where feelings had ceased and mere sensation remained, and even sensation only at a remove, tickling some phantom limb. He had stood there while Lucien loaded up, and then wandered into the fridge and then the freezer for some reason, wanting something to eat, putting things on the ground, forgetting about them, rifling. One image he retained was of Lucien absurdly leaving the walk-in fridge with a large salami under each arm.

Then it was Lucien with two laden clanking bags of wine on the ground before him, but going back for one more he had seen in the fridge because, he said, it was already open so it would go to waste anyway if they didn't have it. Out in the dining room as Richie groped for, dropped, and tried to find the keys, Lucien had stood before the mural which Bella and her friends had painted and laughed at it. He said something mildly disparaging, Richie remembered, though he did not remember exactly what – was it that it was bourgeois? Or boring? Or simply bad, badly rendered? The words were lost but he did remember Lucien uncorking the open bottle of red and pouring it into his hands and flicking it and throwing it at the mural, making some joke, Richie laughing at it, there being a feeling of harmless hyperactive fun. He could just about see the image of the mural with splatters of red wine splayed across it.

There was then an image of being back at Clancy's kitchen table and drawing deeply on the bottle of white wine, which was not even cool as it had been in his thirsty imagination, ash everywhere, the burn in his lungs combined with the acid of the wine deeply satisfying. The girls had gone, he thought. Lucien was putting on more exciting music and was dancing, strutting around the room. Still a feeling of fun, of fuck-what-may-come. There was little concrete after that. Hanging over a toilet, almost-clear vomit. Reaching over and running the shower at full blast to mask the noise.

Once he had got it all out, having a ridiculous thought that if they heard the shower run, they would wonder why he hadn't had a shower. Putting his head under the shower to wet it and make sense of the fact the shower was running. Once he had done that, taking a tube of toothpaste and squirting it into his mouth, putting his mouth to the tap and mixing the two. Collapsing down beside the bath, brain blood pulsing. That for a few minutes and then running the cold tap and shoving his face beneath it. Roaring into the drain to clear his throat. Slapping his face with more water. Going back to the table feeling he had got one over on everyone there, as though they'd never have known what he was doing. Sensation of being annoying, sensation of being pushed into a corner, people laughing. And then nothing until the next day.

5.

In the moment before waking his body was already laden with expansive dread, knowing more than he did. The top part of his chest was so heavy and dense with fright and sorrow that he felt sure he would scream. His pulse thumped disturbingly, erratically, and he put his hand to his throat to touch it, push it back inside of himself. There were too many bad things to think of and he told himself to be calm and slow but it was no use and he sat up on the couch where he lay and put his head in his hands and cried for a few moments. There were two bodies on the other side of the room but they were still and he didn't wake them with his noises.

He needed to know what time it was but he also badly did not want to know. He would have chosen to remain in his brief suspension if it held any comfort at all or the possibility of returning to oblivious sleep but there was no way to move but forward now, the ignorance as excruciating as the truth would be. He turned on the radio to a low volume and waited until he heard what time it was, just after midday. Some of the worst of the alarm had left his body as soon as he knew how bad it was and that nothing could now be salvaged. The lunch party would be arriving, he thought. He hoped that when Bella had come in it had not been so bad that she would have to close for the whole day. He thought of her having to clean up after him. He thought about how much money it might be that he now owed to her. At least the others would help with that. They weren't the worst, it wasn't their fault. It was him. He was the one with the key, the one with that responsibility. She hadn't given a key to Lucien, had she, only to him. He cringed to think of Lucien and their conversation, their chummy familiarity in the dead night. He wondered about the parts he didn't remember.

He rubbed his thumb under his eyes and over his cheeks which he felt to be hot and with the small raised bumps beneath the surface which sometimes came. He knew there was no choice but to go there to the restaurant before he sobered up completely and lost his nerve and would hide from it forever. There were the keys to return and he would have to do that or else she would be frightened he would come back again that night and would need to get the locks changed. The idea of himself as a person to be frightened of was so wrong and obscene, and yet he had to credit it. He could imagine how she would feel after this, because it was how he felt too. He had never felt scared of himself before, that he was a suspect person who couldn't be predicted. He had been sick in the gardens of his friends' parents' houses, and kissed girls he had wished he hadn't, he had been embarrassed plenty, but he had never experienced this depth of shame and total bewilderment at his own actions. He couldn't think about that now.

Around the corner from Mario's he hesitated, and took

the keys out of his pocket to hold them in his hand like a white flag, so that when she saw him she would know he wasn't there to make any further trouble. Outside he winced at the window and shaded his eyes, lingering back in the gutter so as not to cause a scene. Deirdre and Thomas were near the front by the pizza oven, the two teenage romantics he had been laughing about with Bella not that long ago. They stared at him, not with disgust exactly but with frank and indiscreet interest. Is that what sort of person you are?, their expressions seemed to say. Is that what people can be like?

Luke the chef crossed past them and came out of the door, shutting it firmly behind him.

You get out of here now, man, he told Richie.

No I know, I came because I still had the keys. Is Bella here, can you send her out so I can tell her how sorry I am? And that I'll pay her for everything? He looked into the window again and saw that there were customers sitting down which gave him a small sense of relief, and he thought he saw Bella's figure moving in the back.

She won't want to see you. I'll take the keys and I'll make up the bill and make sure you get it. You spoiled a lot of produce too, so it will be a big bill.

Yes, said Richie, almost enjoying the feeling of endless self-loathing reverberating in his chest, glad to have some concrete unpayable debt to focus it on.

Why did you do that? Was it worth it for some party? We had something good between us here and you totally fucked it. There's no point in begging her for your job by the way, I'll quit before I let you work here again.

No, no, of course not. No, it wasn't worth it, and, no, I wouldn't ask for it back. I understand what I've done.

Do you? You really hurt her. This isn't like some corporation where it doesn't matter and what you do doesn't affect anyone. It's her family, and she decided to trust you. To them, it will be like she did this, like she lost the money.

I'll pay the money back, said Richie.

Yeah, yeah, a quid a week for a hundred years? With what will you pay it back? How? He sneered, I'll tell you something now, and it will be the last thing I ever say to you. You want to knock this on the head right now. Today. You don't want to get into habits. You don't want to be the old guys you see with piss dried into their pants sitting at the bar every day of their lives who people don't want to sit near. You're not cut out for it. Some people are, they can handle it and they can stop when they like to. I can tell by the look of you, you don't have the energy to live and to keep behaving like this. It will be one or the other, and you don't have too long to decide which it will be. You're weak. Weak, weak, weak.

As he repeated this he touched Richie's shoulder in a way that indicated solace, but then he turned back around and left him alone and that was as far as the comfort would extend, an appeal for Richie to see how weak he really was.

6.

Richie quit drinking. He went back to his bedroom on Merchant's Quay and he thought about what he had done and what Luke had said to him and why it had to be like this from now on. That first day he felt so abject and exhausted by it, the way his body felt and by the repetition of his life, that it cost him no effort. He tried to speak in his own mind soothingly as he lay in his tomb, wrapping everything tightly, coddling himself like a baby. This was allowable because of the fact he had now given up drinking. He could be kind and tolerant to himself and patient with his body while it healed and restored, because he had stopped. He spoke aloud at times, and thought about that pleasing sentence of childhood, I'm a good person and other people

139

think so too. The sentence helped to calm him because of its habit and rhythm, though if he let himself into the thought for too long it made him panic again, because he couldn't think of anyone who liked him who was not wrong and mistaken to like him.

The next day he gave over to recovery again, believing that on the third day things would be different enough that he could leave the flat, when it was out of his system. There would be new feelings he hadn't experienced in a long time, and plans he wouldn't have been able to make could now be made. This thought, too, was useful as a superficial balm but became an irritant when explored any further. It was impossible to imagine a life which did not involve drinking except for if the Richie in it was an entirely other, new sort of person with traits he had never shared. He allowed himself the faith that he might become that person once he just had a few days off it.

On the third day he felt brighter and went to the house in Mayor's Walk thinking he might see Carmel, but when he arrived and went up to her she was locked in her bedroom and he could hear her muttering something. When he knocked she said she was busy in a vague distracted way. He didn't want to interrupt whatever she was occupied with and left her to it, feeling uncomfortable and unsure about how he should spend the day. He should look for a job, it would relieve him when he was making money and could offer Bella a payment plan, but that prospect and everything it entailed felt as though it might overwhelm the progress he had made. Not for a week, then he would be ready.

He wanted to do something which wasn't like himself, to test the new person he might become, and he borrowed Rose's bicycle, leaving a note to let her know he would be back. He cycled to the promenade in Tramore and then went on a long walk. Memories of childhood surrounded him here, thoughts of Carmel on a tricycle and of eating chips locked in the car in the rain so comfortable and contained. Even his father had sometimes been happy here. A feeling of contentment and buoyancy came over him and he felt proud of himself for not having a drink, and this clean good feeling made him want a drink.

The thought annoyed him and he tried to brush it away, but the contentment persisted and kept suggesting how pleasant it would be in a pub garden. He did not drink that day, but when he returned to the flat he was troubled and went to bed at eight o'clock. When he closed his eyes he thought how lonely he was, and his eyes stung with the thought itself. Loneliness had always existed in two distinct and equally painful dimensions for Richie, once as the missing of people itself, and twice as the idea abstracted. To think of wanting others and not being able to have them was a sad enough concept that it could move him to tears even when he wasn't experiencing it himself, and he was experiencing it himself now. He was alone and he didn't know the man he was renting the room from well enough to burden him with his awkward sober need.

The next day was the fourth day he did not take a drink. It occurred to him to try to access some of the calm he had experienced the day before in Tramore by going again to nature, but this time choosing somewhere less convivial, less full of carousing and less likely to remind him so acutely of wanting to drink. He got a bus to the other seaside village, Dunmore, which had no fairground attractions and was quieter and wealthier. There he wandered a bit to find a mostly isolated beach called Councillors Strand. He sat on a ledge and read his book for a while and then put it away and looked out at the sea, probing himself for peace and revelation. After a long time had passed of examining his emotional state, he grew increasingly despairing. The mood came over him at an elegant, patient pace. He looked at this

141

picture of great, humbling beauty, at the gentle lolloping clouds sliding down into the sunset, and the exquisite peace of the ocean, the sight of the few people still bathing bobbing stoically around, and he felt a devastating lowering within himself.

It was devastating not because it was violent but because it was the very opposite. The feeling was slow and natural and utterly complete. Undeniable, total, and truthful. The feeling was certainty of the essential malevolence of things, certainty that they would only ever be so. There was darkness beneath or inside everything, and even beautiful things were irredeemable because they only acted to obscure but never to transform. The certainty rose and expanded and something changed in him forever as he sensed the indefinite months and years ahead mired in hopelessness. There had been a part of him which was relieved to be admonished by Luke, and told so clearly that drinking was what caused the problems. In this moment on Councillors Strand it became instantly and irrevocably clear that the drinking was only a sideshow. The drinking, the not-drinking, would change nothing of this despair which was a part of him and always would be. It was a terrifying and liberating idea.

In only a few weeks Carmel had gone to England, life in Waterford had come to an end for the family, and it was decided he would leave too. It was Rose who convinced him of this necessity. She put it in terms of practicality, that they would now need the rental income from Mayor's Walk, and he did not have an income or a regular place to stay. Before he got the boat over to join them, he came to an arrangement with himself. When he arrived it would be a new start for him. He wouldn't drink anything he really liked. He would only be allowed red wine and beer. Only the bad stuff, only what he did not like to have. This was the compromise he made, after eighty hours of sobriety, heading into his new life, broken within a month.

Part VI

London, 1990
Hotel Gargano

1.

Tom kept trying to steer their conversation towards the child. Richie had the pig-headed self-obsession that all addicts shared, he thought. He could only speak of things and people as they related to the story of his drinking. He had made as many subtle interjections and thoughtful redirecting questions as it was possible to do without simply screaming at him to shut up and talk about something which mattered. Had he forgotten why they were in this hotel together? Was Carmel the only one of this deranged family clear-headed enough to understand that nobody cared about them, that there was no story besides the death of an infant? The obscenity angered him, though he kept his face smooth and crinkled with empathy as Richie droned on and on. Didn't he understand the extraordinary circumstances, or did children back in Ireland routinely go around smothering one another as a lark?

He supposed that the best way to agitate for anything relevant was to get Richie to say something about himself which indicated embedded familial depravity, which he had so far mostly failed to do. A mildly strained relationship with a stepmother and a rude unemployed father did not lay any substantial groundwork to indicate the inevitability of

145

evil. He dismissed immediately and convincingly the notion that he might know who the secret father of Lucy was, or the details of her conception. He had found out that Carmel was pregnant only after they had already fled in their failed attempt to get her aborted.

When Tom asked him for an impression of what Lucy was like, he was vague and slightly surprised, as though having forgotten he had lived alongside her for her entire life.

She was an awful baby, but I'm sure you've heard that from the neighbours.

Tom, frustrated that this seemed to be the primary summation of the girl from anybody he asked, thought – had none of these people heard a baby cry before? And were they so struck by it that they couldn't forget it a decade later?

It was difficult because Carmel was incapable of taking care of her but Rose didn't want to take over and stop her learning how to, so at first there was this gap, for a few months, where nobody was.

What were you doing at that time, remind me? asked Tom.

A look of offence passed over Richie's face and Tom chided himself to be less flippant. Though Richie was pissed now he was not stupid and no bridges could be burnt before getting something of use.

I was trying to understand what to do with my life, said Richie.

Tom thought, How's that working out for you? and feared the words were close to visible on his face. But it was difficult not to think it. To think that, since Richie had failed about as comprehensively as it was possible to for a man of able body and average intelligence, perhaps his time would have been better used doing what he could to avoid his niece becoming a murderer before she got her first period.

I was twenty-two years old, said Richie, getting agitated. How old are you, Tom, twenty-seven, twenty-eight? What were you like when you were twenty-two? Do you think you would have been enthusiastic about babysitting your sister's kid very much? Were you filled with a sense of community and family duty or were you just doing the best you could and trying to make yourself as happy as possible? That's what I was doing, only I come from what I come from and you're whatever the fuck you are.

What do you mean you come from what you come from? asked Tom.

Nothing. Just, it is what it is.

The magnanimous platitudinous wisdom of the drunk, It is what it is, what will be will be, *carpe diem*, thought Tom.

There is rot in us. I don't know what caused it. I can't name it for you, and isn't that your job anyway? I know it's there. Rose blurred the edges a bit, she wasn't the same as us, and being near Dad only made her more determined to be good, instead of the other way round. Maybe that's why she had to die early, she knew she couldn't keep it at bay forever. When I think of her now I feel so sorry for her. Not because she was miserable because I really don't think she was. I feel sorry for her because she had no personality. She wasn't allowed one, because she had to be good, good, good, to make up for the rest of us. Before we moved here she still had some of her own self. You could see it with her friends and sometimes with Carmel, but then she had to be nothing but good until she died.

Tom thought about this.

You mentioned before that your father liked to keep you and Rose separate from one another. Why do you think he did that? What do you think he was feeling when he did that?

Ask him, said Richie.

I will ask him. Absolutely I'll ask him. But I'd like to know what your opinion is too. It doesn't make much sense to me that he liked to keep someone as benevolent but also as useful as Rose away from you, do you see what I mean?

147

If he wasn't able to connect with you for whatever reason, surely it would have made sense for him to have someone who could mother you involved, instead of himself? Surely that was part of why he got together with Rose when you were so young?

There were a few moments of silence in the room, except for Richie's rapid thready breath, the sound of which made Tom think that Richie was very upset and also more physically compromised than Tom had first noticed.

I learned very young not to bother trying to look into his head. I'll be impressed if you get even the faintest insight when you talk to him. There were so few times he gave me anything to work with. There were fights, but what can you learn from somebody telling you to stop robbing their drink or putting their clothes in the wrong drawers? He was just a vacuum, there was nothing.

But there was. There was a time when there was something more than absence. He thought about it for a moment, about whether to say it, and Tom allowed him to take the time, and in the end he did, although he was as unsure as he ever was about what it meant, if it meant anything at all.

2.

Richie was fifteen and had been at a party until dawn. He was new to passing out and didn't realise how easily it could happen after a certain amount of drinking. When he got home in the early hours of the morning and tried to open the toilet door he was unable to. Thinking, wrongly, there was somebody in there already (in fact he needed only to shoulder the lock slightly as he knew automatically to do in his sober, waking life), he had lain down on the long bench in the hall which was between the bathroom and the bedrooms, planning to rest for a moment until whatever occupier of the toilet emerged. Instead, he fell asleep.

Rose woke earlier than anyone else in the house, and because this was true she often padded out to the bathroom still half asleep and not always fully dressed if she happened to have slept that way. It was just a habit, one not questioned or noticed by herself or anyone else because she never coincided with anyone.

While Richie slept on the bench, Rose opened her bedroom door wearing only a pair of knickers and took a few bleary steps before the substantial bulk of a teenage boy emerged in her peripheral vision and she screamed. Immediately after that, she realised it was him and screamed a second time, For God's sake Richie! before running back into her room and slamming the door behind her. Richie had been startled comprehensively out of sleep but only by the noise and he had not even registered that Rose was undressed. She began to laugh behind the door and said, I'll kill you you dopey little fucker, you gave me the fright of my life.

He laughed back and said he was sorry, fully awake now and stretching his stiff body, any threat of a hangover instantaneously dispelled from the shock. He got a glass of water and then went into the sitting room. A few moments later his father walked in with a look of unhinged rage.

Were you looking at my wife?

What?

I said, were you looking at my wife – you disgusting little prick. You pervert, you ungrateful little shit.

He reached out and with his good arm took Richie by the throat and even through the surprise he couldn't help but take in the exotic proximity of his father – the smell of his face! The unknown colours of his most intimate tiny hairs!

Dad, no. No. Of course I wasn't. I just fell asleep there, I didn't even see her.

The words weren't entering his father at all.

I know you. I know what you are. I know people like you, he said, still horribly, wonderfully close to Richie's face, who now began trying gently to extricate himself.

I didn't do anything. Ask her yourself. He stopped and listened as though Rose would interject of her own accord. But there was no noise, nothing from the direction of Rose, and Richie worried now.

In the bedroom Rose stood frozen, tuning out the sound of the men and listening only for Carmel's movement. She pressed her ear on the wall toward her own child's room and heard that she was still, no rustling or confused cries, and remained there willing her continued sleep. As long as there was no sound from that direction things would be alright.

You'll get down on your knees and ask me for forgiveness, said John. And it was so absurd – this father whose silence, for their whole lives, his silence had been a wound Richie thought he might never recover from – it was so absurd for him to be speaking in this way, for him to ask to be spoken to in this way, like they were in some play where fathers and sons said such things to one another.

He didn't laugh, but nor did he do it, which he would be thankful for. It was possible it could have gone another way, only that he was able to think of Rose laughing a few minutes beforehand and assure himself he had not transgressed.

No I won't do that, he said, apologetically, and waited to be hit, but his father only set his jaw and gave him a final squeeze around the throat and told him to be careful how he behaved in this house. Which he was already and had always been.

The incident was never mentioned by either of them again, or by Rose. There were times it churned in Richie to say something to her, to make a joke about it, or to sit her down and make sure they were all square. In moments of even natural silence between them in the house he sometimes fairly burst to ask that she held no suspicion or resentment about that morning, but the moments passed quickly and without notice. Her reliable, insistent pleasantness forbade confrontation. It did not allow the minor bubbles of discomfort between them remain long enough to aerate fully, to sour into actual animosity which might have lent momentum.

So he did not ask her but sometimes the thought of it came to him in the night or in the first gasp of a desperate morning, as a spark of potential shame so humbling he had to press his fingers into his eyes to make it disappear. The event shifted and blurred over the years as he grew further away from the young drunk boy who experienced it. The face of his father, though – that face which had become suddenly lively and beautiful with brutality as it otherwise never was – remained vivid in his memory.

This discrepancy between the blurriness of the event and the complete certainty of the resulting rage meant that he did wonder occasionally if he had been somehow in the wrong. He had done much worse things while drunk since then, but he felt that his genuine lack of sexual curiosity about Rose, that he experienced the same familial repulsion toward her he did all female relatives, gave his version credence. There was simply no way to know, and now she was dead and the idea of bringing it up with his father was as alienatingly melodramatic as the argument itself. These were things that other kinds of people did, things for the verbal and fortunate.

3.

It was a story with as little dramatic force as most of Richie's meandering yarns, Tom thought, and yet it did summon some compelling questions and thoughts by association.

The actual occurrence could be spun into something of use if he needed it to take up space (Uncle of Kid Killer was Peeping Tom as a Teen – To his Own Stepmum!) but more crucially it suggested disturbing family dynamics. What sort of father was romantically jealous of his own teenage son? What did that say about the way John engaged with his family as a whole? At the very least it implied a furthering of the ordinary ownership a man felt over his children into unusual sexualised territory, and even the suggestion of this convergence would go a long way.

Now he had an angle in mind for when he spoke to John, and to Carmel, new things to be careful of and to broach. The story did, too, raise the question of what sort of man Richie really was. There had been no real talk of women in his life aside from a teenage casual girlfriend. If there was anything untoward about him, and he had grown up alongside not only Carmel but Lucy herself, that would be interesting. He excused himself and downstairs picked up the phone to organise a reporter who could get to Waterford quickly and start asking questions.

When he returned, he asked Richie, What do you mean, when you say you've done much worse things while drunk than that, than to look at Rose? What worse things? In London, you mean?

Yeah, said Richie, hoarse. Worse things in London.

Tell me, Richie.

Just – Lucy, he began and then started to cry. Tom looked on trying not to let his benevolence slip, to betray his disgust.

Lucy? he goaded kindly.

It's hard to talk about it.

I know it is.

She was alone all the time. Carmel went to work, she did a mix of afternoon and overnights, and Dad would disappear or wouldn't respond so she'd ask me to look after the kid. I did sometimes, but then things started going. I was losing time in a way I didn't before, and I'd wake up sometimes the next day and not know where she was or what had happened the whole day and night. Every time, I checked on her and it was fine, Carmel was home and Lucy was still alive and even though I couldn't remember, nothing bad had happened, that I could see. I just couldn't remember.

The day Mia went missing I was supposed to be looking after Lucy. I remember giving her breakfast – I hadn't been to sleep – and the next thing I remember it was the middle of the night and I could hear all the – all the excitement, in the square. I went out to the balcony and tried to hear what they were saying below, and everyone was talking about the little girl going missing. I knew. I thought I knew, it had happened at last, that she was dead and it was my fault. I tore in to check the bed and she was there, tucked up and fine, but this time that didn't make me feel better. All those hours were gone, and something terrible had happened. Finally. The relief that Lucy was alright, but then the sickness of the little girl being gone, the not remembering. I can't remember. I'm so ashamed all of the time.

He repeated several times, shrill, I can't remember, I can't remember.

Good enough, thought Tom.

4.

It was funny, John thought, what you passed on.

He was shortly after finishing his lunch, a plate of limp, steaming fish and chips brought up to the room beneath a silver dome which was then removed with a jarringly elegant flourish by the hotel proprietor. He ate with brusque rapidity. In the same moment as he put the last forkful into his mouth, he stood and pushed the remains from the plate into a small bedside bin with three swift movements. Then, automatically, he put the empty plate back on its tray and beneath its dome and placed it outside the door where he wouldn't be aware of it any more.

Yes, it was funny, he thought as he lay down on the bed digesting, clear now of the mental clutter of dining.

His way of eating had never felt remarkable to him. Indeed he wouldn't have guessed that he had a specific way of eating, or that anyone did. It was only clarified for him once, when Carmel was ten and Richie fifteen. (It wasn't long before that incident with Richie looking at Rose which still filled him with muddled but visceral and burning outrage to this day – the drunken gawping leer of the boy as he watched his wife in her knickers. Although, he corrected himself, could it have been that way exactly, because hadn't he only seen Richie after Rose woke them all up shouting? Could he have seen the expression Richie wore as he did it? It didn't matter; he had seen the smug laughter on his face after he had done it. That was good enough, alright.)

They had finished eating their dinners except for Rose who was always the last, languidly slicing up little bits and combining them in various configurations almost like she was annoying them on purpose with her idle refusal to be through with it. The rest of them anxiously waited at the table, forbidden from abandoning it until everyone was done. They were, though, allowed to clear their plates as soon as they finished eating, because the three of them visibly shook to do so otherwise and it irritated her.

Why is it you're always the only one still eating at the end, Mam? asked Carmel.

You and Richie took up your father's ways, that's all Car, she told her.

And John had looked at her and jerked his head to the side to make a question mark.

154

Some people sit for hours over dinner, Rose explained, and they don't mind sitting at the table while it still has food on it even after they stop eating. I went to Paris the summer after I finished school on a holiday with my sister Fiona and her husband, and people sat around all night with the dinner still all over the place. She sounded wistful and fond. We went to a party at his friend's flat and stayed up until three o'clock in the morning drinking at the table with chicken and bread and bits still on it. A girl was ashing into a tray with olives in it and I ate one by mistake.

Carmel was impatient, the story not to her liking. She did not enjoy to hear about anything Rose had done before she met her father. (Nor did she like to hear about Richie's mother Louise or anything of John's life with her. It was uncomfortable to think she might so nearly not have existed.)

Yeah, but why does Daddy do it that way and you don't?

Oh I don't know Carmel, said Rose, standing up with her plate and losing patience with the conversation. When your granny June, Daddy's mother, was still alive she used to do it the same way. Probably something she picked up in the poorhouse and handed down.

John was astonished by this throwaway observation from Rose who had only met his mother twice before she died. He cleared his throat and stood up to help with the dishes. He had never thought of it, but this was true. His mother was an even more ruthlessly efficient eater than himself and always had been, managing to not only clear but also wash and dry a plate she was using within five minutes of having sat down to dinner. And of course it made sense that she would have learned to eat as quickly as she could, and to remove all trace of having done so, in that kind of place she grew up in. His eyes stung at the thought of her as a child learning not to let anyone know she existed. To think he could have these big confident bold children swaggering around in the 1970s and they

155

could still be living out ways the nuns had forced into his mother before the turn of the century. He thought that he might make an effort to slow down at mealtimes and show them he could relax so that they would let themselves too, and Rose might enjoy herself more. Soon Richie stopped being around for meals anyway and the pursuit of the long conversational dinner seemed a lost cause belonging to another time.

Tom, the boy from the newspaper, had come into his bedroom now and was pouring more drinks and settling in to interrogate. His manner had changed since the night before. He spoke faster, with less kindness and cautious hesitation. He asked question after question about what sort of child Lucy was, which John knew better than to answer and ignored totally. He may be drunk but he was not drunk enough to ruin Lucy's life with a careless comment. What a mess it was. He could not think of it.

Why would Lucy be inclined to hurt another child, do you think, John? and when John didn't respond he sounded angry and said, You lived with her for ten years for God's sake, you all did, don't you have anything to say about her? Was she even there? Were you?

It was a good question, in fairness to the boy. Were they there at all? The night before, when the pain and dread of what had happened was settling on his chest and preventing sleep, John had tried to think through the past ten years. It had all seemed nonsensical when he recited it to himself. How had he come to live in England, old enemy England, at his late age, and never having thought of it one way or another for his whole life except with mild mockery when men he knew came back tail between their legs after a few years trying and failing here? There was no reasonable explanation for it except that Rose had told him to and she hadn't presented it as a choice, and her instructions were always good ones to that point.

The years afterward had passed with bewildering speed as he watched her try to cope and strategise what the baby needed and what Carmel needed and seemed never to be content that she was doing enough for either of them. He couldn't say much about how Lucy was back then because he was only watching her through Rose's panicked eyes, and when she did well he was pleased because Rose was pleased, and when she was bad he was unhappy because Rose was unhappy. And it was most definitely true that he did not know what had become of Lucy in the time since Rose was ill and died, because after that he had lived consciously in a hinterland, marking days with joyless determination until it was the right time to die or go back to Waterford. He longed with a passion that surprised himself to go home and live there before the end of his life. He had promised her near her death that he would stay in London until the children were out of the flat and able to take care of themselves, and he hadn't been able to break this promise, although neither was he able to do anything that might have helped them in this aim. He waited, expecting they would do something to themselves in some way or another. Which, now, in a way, one of them had; he had not expected it to be Lucy.

Tom was still going on and on, sounding more annoyed. What had Richie said to this fellow to get him in such bad humour? He laughed at the thought of what rubbish his son may have come out with. Tom watched him do so in silence. An old man flat on his back on a bed, laughing, being watched over by a stern Englishman in an armchair. What a life this was. A thought which made him think of how his mother would say, whenever the two of them were doing a pleasant task, or when the weather was fine, Ah, if this isn't living, then what is – filling jars with blackberry jam and sealing them, sitting on the bench near the courthouse when the sun was going down, skimming stones on Councillors

Strand in Dunmore, Ah, if this isn't living then what is, they would ask each other.

He found it difficult to focus on what the English boy was saying, his head was swimming and he was trying to remember too many things at once. It seemed very important suddenly that the boy know about his mother, that he might print something in the paper about her and the things she overcame and what a nice time they had had together during his childhood despite it all. While he was deciding how to tell him this, he concentrated back in on what it was Tom was going on about.

He was asking now about Carmel's sex life. Asking, was he sure he didn't know who Lucy's father was, how could he not have known who his own daughter was sleeping with, while she lived under his roof? Mother of God, was there no end to it, the sex? Somehow it had ruined his life several times over, although it had never particularly moved him personally one way or the other. There had of course been the final ruin of Carmel and the surreal nightmare of her hidden love life, its sudden eruption. Her moments of indiscretion which had fractured life into distinct parts, her urges and their outcomes which had brought them to this foreign place to be destroyed one by one. But before that, before Carmel existed and before Rose, there had been his wife Louise whose private outlets ruined him for the first time.

He loved Louise fully and fiercely, slight little feathery thing that she was, the top of her strawberry-blonde head barely coming up to his biceps. Her cautious, precise elegance and tiny body made him feel pleasantly like an oafish, bounding dog. He loved her with the unwavering arrogance of one who expects their love to go on forever without question, and there was no reason he ought to have questioned it. It had never happened to anyone he had ever known, nor even heard of, that their wife left one day just because she didn't fancy having a family any longer, because she valued sex – sex with anybody, lots of people, anyone who would have her, people said – more than them. It had never been known to happen, not in Waterford, not in Ireland, quite possibly in the history of human relations, until it happened to him.

She was his first everything, when they met at seventeen. She said that he was hers too but he had to recast it all after she left and doubt each part individually. It seemed unlikely, bearing in mind what her true nature was revealed to be, that it was really her first time that blushing evening when she ushered him in through the back of the house when her parents were away in their camper for the night and they undressed each other in holy silence in her bedroom with a framed painting of St Teresa hanging over them. He had no reason to disbelieve her then, and wouldn't have thought to. She was a gorgeous singer, the star of the choir in the Sacred Heart, and she would idly burst into whatever song was in her head while she did errands or walked through town (he might have known, he would think ruefully in future, that she was growing bored with him when she sang a few bars of something one evening in bed as he held her and put his hands fondly over her breasts).

They married straight out of school and rented the house on Mayor's Walk and for a while lived in an almost nauseating state of happiness. They were too young to feel that happiness held any stakes and too stupid to fear its loss. They had sex often enough, it felt to John, which was once or twice a week. He liked to do it and needed no convincing, but it was not the core part of his love for her, just a pleasant additional confirmation of it. He was as happy about the moments before and after the act, as happy about any time he could be completely close to her. This was what he valued the most, to be alone together and have no shame or qualms about the limitless amount of closeness he needed

159

from her. At night when they turned to sleep, he surrounded her so totally and firmly that she would be gasping and overheated soon after and would have to extricate herself from his clinging grip. In the early time she would laugh kindly as she did this and remove his limbs patiently, rearranging them into something more accommodating for her comfort. Later, when it was getting bad, she would rise up from her position amongst his sprawled parts and scream with repelled frustration, I can't breathe.

Louise had wanted to have children right away but he put her off, saying he wanted to be earning better money first, to aim for management in the meat-processing plant where he worked. This was only part of the truth – he was in fact a competent and amiable but lazy worker – and the whole of it was that he prized his life alone with her so extremely that he wasn't willing to give it up straight away. He had only just left the house he shared with his mother, and while her sturdy self-sufficiency could never be misconstrued as needy, he had nevertheless felt all his life the burden of giving her joy, of being a good boy to and for her. He didn't want to owe things to others just yet, not while he was able to feel the free and uncomplicated exchange of pleasure and company between himself and his wife. They had long, full decades stretching out before them which they would spend with their children, after they had had their own time.

He didn't care for going out as she did. He had never had many friends, and expected when he married it was the end to the mild discomfort of that absence. He had a drink on Fridays with some of the men from work which he mostly enjoyed and was home by eight, ready to be alone with her. He took her out when she asked, but wouldn't have thought to if she didn't. He didn't understand why she longed so badly to get dressed up and put make-up on on weekend nights, or why she wanted to go out to have a meal and a

160

drink with him since they could do the same thing at home with nobody watching it. The pleasure he took from her was diminished by it being witnessed, but hers was increased. She became irritable about his carelessness of appearance when she wanted to go out. She had always praised his looks, which were pronounced and noble if not especially handsome, but now gave out about his bad posture and uncut fingernails and half-grown-in beard, which she complained was too many different colours – How can one man be blond-, black- and red-haired in the same face? she said despairingly.

She had worked two days a week in the cake shop since she was fifteen, and went up now to three days and Saturday mornings because she said she was bored while he was working, if they weren't going to have children then there was little enough to do in the house to keep it well.

Why Saturdays then? he asked. If it's because you're bored, why do the Saturday, I'm home then aren't I?

Because, she told him crossly, Saturdays are the most fun, and you see the most people.

She began then to go out without him, with, she said, the other girls from the shop, and sometimes their boyfriends. He asked if he should come as well, seeing as their men were.

Oh, don't, John, I know you don't want to and I don't need you sitting there all night making me feel like I have to go any second or else you'll be bored.

Which, he felt, was reasonable, and didn't make him unhappy at first. He did miss her, but she was right that he preferred to be in and miss her than out with her and the others. Usually he went down the road to spend the evening with his mother those nights, the two of them did a puzzle and ate dinner together, and if his mother thought it odd that a couple two years into their marriage spent two nights a week on average apart, she didn't mention anything. At

161

first it was never terribly late when she got in and she wasn't ever too drunk, it felt cosy to welcome her into the warm bed where he sat doing a crossword or reading the paper, her smelling all of cold and outside and tobacco and talcum.

The first really bad time was on a Saturday. She had told him in advance that she wouldn't be back straight away after the shift because it was someone's birthday and they were going out to lunch. Mindlessly – and mildly – he said to her not to spend too much money, and this was only because of his perception, given to him by his mother and upbringing, that restaurants were for the rich and foolish.

They are my wages, if you remember, she had said to him, standing very still in their kitchen, her arms crossed tightly, rigid with annoyance. Don't you think I can do what I like with my own wages?

Hey now, hey now, okay, he said, trying to make it a joke instantly, but also slightly angry himself. Don't act like I make you go out and earn them. We have enough with my job for you to stay home if you'd rather.

Stay home and do what? Dust the tiny house which is already clean? Arrange your shoes? Or just sit and wait for you to come back and miss you?

Which was a painful thing to say as they both knew this was what he wanted in his truest most private self. Even if it was an indefensible thing to want he would never have asked for it to happen, so it seemed cruel to mock his crude, childish heart.

She left and did not return until midnight, the lunch having been arranged for 2 p.m. She smelled spicy and unfamiliar and was so drunk she couldn't stand. This was pathetic and fairly comic and he wasn't able to be angry – her sweet little bones clattering off surfaces as she bounced around grasping for unknown things.

Okay love, let's go to bed, he said.

162

Lots of people want to go to bed with me, she said, looking at him with spiteful bravado.

What are you talking about, Lou? he said. You're pissed, you don't know what you're on about.

Yes, I do. You aren't bothered about going to bed with me, but there are others who do want to. Who would like to, very much, take me to bed, if you won't.

He was too disturbed to hear more, and put her in on the couch and took her shoes off and a blanket over her and some water beside her.

I'll ask her in the morning what she meant by that, he thought to himself as he climbed the stairs to their bed, but in the morning a great fear came over him and he could neither ask her nor speak at all for the rest of the day.

5.

A contract of silence was established between them, under which it was agreed that if she treated him kindly and did not come home at objectionable times then he would say nothing about her being out without him two, three, sometimes four nights a week. It was easy not to think anything of it, because she always slept at home with him. Once, for a week, the phone rang at odd times and sometimes the caller hung up after only a few seconds, and sometimes hung up only when he answered the phone. He heard her answer it herself one night and shout, Hello? Hello? with the same baffled frustration as he did, which eased his slight suspicion.

She asked him occasionally for children but he had never felt even a mild stir of desire for one and put her off as he always had done. She asked it less and less, and when she did so he sensed that she was doing so out of habit or duty instead of anything deeply heartfelt. They both kept to their terms more or less consistently, although occasionally there would be some special night out for a birthday or around Christmas and she would come home in a state as she had that first Saturday. On these nights she menaced him, taunting him, and eventually taking to pushing him and scratching his face when he refused to participate in her theatre. She broke plates, glasses, remembering nothing of it in the morning, when she was sorry and soft and clung back to him when he grabbed her tightly in the bed. He loved her as fiercely and plainly as he ever had.

Those events were sparse enough that they went on for several years in their uneasy truce, and may have continued to do so forever if not for the accident and what came afterwards. It was a freak thing, the sort which arose every few years at the processing plant; he had leaned forward to pick up a box to clear a jam when his jacket got caught in a roller. As he tried to pull it out his hand was drawn in too, instantly crushing it and his forearm. A man on the sanitation crew had seen it happen immediately and managed to switch the machine off, sparing John amputation or damage higher up his arm. Instead, the arm was simply left withered and useless. The company paid him a one-off compensation quickly and quietly to avoid a court case or more extensive publicity, of an amount they impressed upon him would be enough to buy the house he rented in Mayor's Walk outright, which he did. He would be on disability payments for the foreseeable, although they also told him they would be open to interviewing him for certain kinds of office positions should they arise.

Louise reminded him of this offer when he appeared to be sinking into a new and unmanageable sort of depression, but he knew from the beginning that he would never return to that place. He felt dirtied by the incident somehow, as though the mild deformity of his injuries meant that he was inherently loathsome, as though that shame reached back in time to make him to blame for the accident which caused it, he was host to an ugliness so great that it retrospectively justified its own cause. He had a strange, secret inclination that the injury was inevitable and revealed him to have been deserving of pain and punishment for his entire life in a way which had only now come to be satisfied, but had been obvious to everyone but him all along. The idea of being a sort of pitiable and functionally useless office boy was too intolerable to consider. He couldn't type, had not been able to before the accident either, and even making a round of tea would take him longer than your average idiot they could hire off the street. It was not possible to bear. They survived easily enough between his dole and Louise's work.

He was seized sometimes by an irritable sort of unhappiness for which he could find no consolation until he thought seriously for the first time about having a child, the idea of which then crashed over his body in a wave of relief as though he was the first person to ever have considered it and was a genius for having done so. There would be a direction and a point to the rest of his life beyond loving Louise and his mother now, after all. He could do something good for both of them, giving Louise the child she had asked for, and his mother a dose of pure uncomplicated familial love to enjoy in her later years. He could facilitate a childhood which was unusually rich with attention. He could correct some of the wrongs of his own life by being a father he hadn't had himself. He could think of every niggling little gap which had arisen in his childhood and preemptively fill it for this new child, this lucky, lucky child, and in doing so perhaps even parent himself back into full health.

When he brought the idea to Louise while they were out for a drink on a Friday evening she was sedate, but she did not seem surprised. Afterward he would think she had the air of one who had been waiting for him to arrive to this necessary conclusion alone, but had been quietly dreading it. She agreed that it was the time to do it, before it got too late.

You look fifteen still, he said to her ruffling her hair.

She patted it down smoothly and said, I'm not though. I'm getting old, John, and then drank deeply from her glass and looked around herself a little wildly, as though afraid someone would hear her or come and bundle her away for admitting the sin of ageing.

We're not old, he said, baffled, for they were only twenty-one.

It's different for men, she said with a small self-pitying smile which she offered to him in forgiveness of his ignorance.

The phone began to ring again a month later, coming at all hours now and waking them up in the dead of night and disturbing them in the middle of their careful lovemaking. John checked with his mother she wasn't having trouble trying to contact him, and wondered to Louise if they should ask his friend Arthur Daly the Garda if they should worry about it. Don't bother Arthur over nothing, it would be more in your line to get the number changed, Louise said.

And he did this and the calls didn't start up again for several months, by which time Louise was pregnant and he was laden with sentimental worship for her and the future she bore. When they began again they came only during the day, and only when Louise was working in the cake shop. The first of these he answered while polishing his good shoes for a wedding they had on in Kilmacthomas the following day.

John Green? the voice asked uncertainly.

Speaking, he said back, with a good amount of idle cheer.

The voice changed, hissing and forceful. Everybody fucks your wife, it said, and then hung up.

He stood in the sitting room next to the television and

166

the window, where the phone was fixed to the wall, with the receiver lodged between his jaw and his shoulder, hand free to hold its hopeful polish. He didn't move for several seconds after the voice had hung up, stunned by the insane brutality of its words. Everybody fucks your wife. 'Fucks your wife' was surely a bad enough combination of words on its own, but it was rendered truly bizarre by the unlikely addition of 'everybody'. He hung up the phone and then after a moment took it off its hook and left it to dangle, in case it might go off again.

He sat down, trying to think of something to explain to himself. It was amazing the way the body worked, that it could change in its entirety in just one second. Before he had picked up the call he had felt ravenously hungry and was amusing himself while he polished the shoes by running through all the various things he might consider eating for lunch. Now, his stomach was scarcely perceptible beneath the teeming flurry of panic which filled his whole centre. He put a hand on his chest trying to ground himself, and thought of the words 'nervous system'. He had thought of nerves quite frequently since his accident, because of some of those in his hand being demolished, but he had never felt aware before of having a nervous system. He thought of how his mother would say about her friends and neighbours that some of them 'suffered from nerves' and he saw now how dully literal that phrasing really was. He could feel signals firing off into every part of his body, trying to warn his brain that something was terribly wrong. All of this was happening because of four words spoken to him at midday on a Thursday.

It was so fantastically awful that there was no way to tell Louise about it. He felt something akin to the shame which had afflicted him after his accident, that only a person as uniquely and mysteriously awful as himself could have been subject to those words – that he would be poisoning Louise

167

by repeating them to her. He said nothing, and they went to the wedding together which was that of Louise's colleague Thomas McCarthy and which was the beneficiary of unexpected and spectacular sunshine. He behaved naturally, quiet but jovial, and found that he was even able to almost enjoy the day. The phone call was too bad to be real except when he was alone, during which moments he panicked and had to immediately find Louise and grasp her tightly and talk loudly about her pregnancy.

6.

The calls came once or twice a week for the following three months. Each time it was a similar but varied phrase; once it was 'We all fuck your wife,' and another time 'Louise loves to be fucked by us.' It was, he felt certain, the same person hissing each time, but they spoke in the royal We as though representing a broad panel of experts on fucking his wife. Having not disclosed his experience to Louise when it happened first, it became impossible to contemplate doing so. Each time he had not spoken of the betrayal, he became further complicit in it. He had grown practically accustomed to receiving and instantly attempting to repress the calls. In moments when lucidity threatened to overwhelm him and make him confront the situation, he reminded himself it may be very dangerous to cause a pregnant woman stress. He taught himself to think only of reaching the end point of the baby's birth. He did not allow himself any room to dwell in the meaning of the calls, and instead dealt exclusively in the physical side effects of incessant denial, which were constant and disgusting. As well as the surge of nauseating adrenaline he experienced in the moment, the reverberations thereafter had caused an ongoing and repulsive stomach complaint. Several times a week when he went to the toilet he saw a reasonable amount of blood in his stool and sometimes wept with panic before pushing that down too with his psychotic pragmatism.

Finally the birth came, and in the intensity of those hours and the long night when he first held his son, all other concerns really did seem pathetic and frivolous. Only hours after they had arrived home, the three of them, the phone rang and when he picked it up and it began spewing its bile he left it off the hook and said to her without forethought, as she nursed the baby: Is there someone else, Louise?

She looked up at him with a look of admonishment and shushed him vaguely, indicating the child.

What do you mean, John? Do be quiet will you.

Is there someone else you're seeing? Romantically?

Well not right now, obviously.

And that was the end of everything – how casually she said it.

I'm a bit busy just at the moment for seeing anyone, she said, almost laughing, or maybe it was just a glow of fondness from looking down at her baby.

But you have been, before this, been seeing someone?

She looked at him quizzically, with a bit of scorn. Are you joking?

No, I'm certainly not joking, are you? he said, trying to keep his voice low.

Yeah, I was seeing someone, and someone else before him. You know this.

I don't know this, he said helplessly, utterly lost and exhausted from his months of careful, forceful resistance being undone in moments, without hesitation. Are you saying . . . is the baby mine? he made himself ask.

Jesus, yes he's all yours alright. I haven't seen anyone since we decided to have him, but even before that I was always careful with anyone else. John, you know this, have you gone mad? Did something happen?

He still could not bring himself to describe the phone calls.

John, but I thought we sorted this out years ago. You only want to go to bed with me three times a year. I thought we had an agreement that we would keep our life here going, and I would do my own thing sometimes. Obviously things will change now the baby is here, that's only natural.

She was distracted again so easily that he saw it was actually true, that she had been used to this arrangement for years, an arrangement he had not known he was part of. She was looking down at the baby again, delighted, obsessed.

What will we call him, eh? she said, and started murmuring boys' names into the child's face.

It did not take so long until the force of her obsession wore thin and she wanted to go out again. Knowing the truth now, and with Richard in the house still so tiny and helpless without her, John established a zero-tolerance situation, and then before the boy turned one she had disappeared and left them both. There was only a half-hearted apology note which mentioned England and a vague promise to get in touch to arrange visits. John left Mayor's Walk and took the baby to his mother's house, where they would stay until he met Rose a year later, whom he latched onto with total relief, total reliance. Rose was older than she wanted to be getting married and beginning to panic. She was desperate to get out of her family house and perhaps because of these things wasn't put off by the prospect of raising another woman's child. When she struggled with it she pretended in her mind that Louise was dead, for who would begrudge raising a dead woman's child, and soon it was the truth anyway although they didn't know it right away. He heard only years later that she had died in England very young of ovarian cancer, or womb, something to do with her reproductive parts, and he thought to himself just once with heady sadism that that was what she got, that

170

her disgusting, incontinent sexuality had poisoned her womanly parts and killed her.

That was what sex had done to him, to his life, to his family. And now this newspaper fellow sat there wanting to shoot the breeze about how it all worked? He was asking and asking about Lucy's father, asking about Richie and Carmel sharing a room. What was he getting at? They shared a room because there were only the two bedrooms. He tried to explain the layout of the house to him, he was telling him facts about the condition the place was in when he had first bought it, he was saying he would love to get back over to it, and he spoke this way until he was asleep and snoring.

Part VII

London, 1990

1.

The old man had spoken near-gibberish for an hour before passing out cold. Tom had tried to steer him in a useful direction but he had gone right on with whatever he was stuck on about his first wife, who was completely irrelevant to Tom's story. He left the room in righteous disgust but that feeling quickly failed him as the reality of the situation established itself back in his room. He had practically nothing of any use so far. Some fairly banal stories about Lucy smacking a kid in school, whispers from neighbours about how infrequently the fucking bins were put out. None of it was any good to him. He only had Carmel left to give him anything. She was going to be tired and upset from having seen Lucy kept captive in the station earlier, surely. It was possible he just needed to press her a bit and everything would come out of her, and then everything would turn out just fine for him. There was also a freelance hack touching down in Waterford at midnight who would spend the next day combing the town for any archaic gossip about John or illuminating stories of the younger Greens. Between the two of them they would cobble something substantial together, something to make a splash with before the other papers got something.

You have the girl here, he told himself, use her.

There had to be something to explain an act of violence like this, to explain a child like Lucy. There had to be something Carmel would say to make some sense of it. That's what she will want to do, he thought, she will want to give an excuse so that Lucy isn't evil, so she hasn't produced an evil child. She wants an excuse – so let her have one. Open up the floor.

2.

Her room was dimly lit by a lamp with a towel flung over the top. After she let him in and then went into the bathroom to wash her face he moved the towel away fearing fire, then thought helplessly 'DISCO INFERNO! Family of Kid Killer Drink All Night Before Deadly Blaze'.

There were things flung across every surface, which was an achievement as her only belongings were the bag of matronly clothing and underwear Jean the secretary had bought for her. Every item had been taken out and apparently found wanting. She wore her own clothes and, he gathered from a very quick survey of the number of sturdy white bras and knickers with tags still attached strewn across the desk and the bed, she was likely also still wearing the underwear she had arrived in.

Sorry, she said, when she came back out, gesturing at it all and then clearing it into a single mound, I was in a bit of a panic this morning, I woke up late to go to the station.

Tom had worked himself, intentionally, into a hyperactive determined mania before he came to her, knowing this was possibly his last chance to get something, and now found he had to slow himself down to match her energy. She was different from the quick-witted and sharp, abrasive woman he had met the night before, and the haughty one her neighbours spoke of. She wasn't making eye contact

176

with him, her matted hair falling down across her face, looking softened, beaten. Good.

She made enough space for them to sit at the desk together and he scooted his chair closer to join her there.

Drink? he asked.

She nodded, weary. Just some wine please, red, and as he took the corkscrew to open it she said apologetically, I don't drink like the other two. Well, obviously I don't drink like Richie, but not even quite a lot like my father.

She said it like he would have been hoping for her to drink a lot, and knew his malevolent reasons for that hope, but didn't actually blame him or mind much. He was glad now that she wasn't a drunk. Her brother and father had been too consumed by their own historical injustices to reveal anything. It was possible this new downtrodden lucidity of hers would prove much more useful.

He asked her why she didn't drink so much. She told him that growing up around Richie had been something of a deterrent but that there had been one time in her life when she drank a lot, every day, and the notion of drinking had become stitched into the misery of that time.

When was that? he asked gently, sipping his wine with sympathetic moderation.

Ah. It was when I was pregnant. But I sort of didn't know I was pregnant, even after I found out. It wasn't real, or something like that, until other people knew, and by then it was too late.

She said this with composure but while biting back her wavering bottom lip which threatened to give more of herself away. Tom felt a gnawing ache in his chest at the erotic combination of her despair and her beauty. There was something about being on the brink of ruin or madness that had something in common with the precious, charged euphoria of the moments before you made a move on somebody. That capitulation, the abandon, the will to shake the rest of life away and admit it could no longer be helped. He had the sudden insane urge to tell her that he loved her, which he resisted, instead gently inviting her to explain further about that time in her life and the pregnancy.

She told him, astonishing herself, speaking things aloud she never had before, things she had scarcely even thought in the privacy of her own head before.

Something had been shaken loose in her to see Lucy in the police station content and autonomous and the subject of attention from so many strangers. The thing they thought she had done was so enormous and so dreadful, if it was true then Lucy would have been responsible for having hurt and interested such a great many people. This was not to say that Carmel had accepted it was true – but even the suspicion of it, even the remotest possibility, had forced her to see for the first time that Lucy was a person who was both real and separate from herself.

She had believed in the separation all along, had put all her faith in the fact that she was not bound to or a part of this stranger child, but she was capable of doing this only because she was incapable of also considering her to be real. She had kept her in her head as the physiologically alive but meaningfully redundant presence she had felt her to be as a fetus. And it had not become pronounced yet but she could feel the possibility that Lucy's unreality to her was only the worst of a whole universe of unreal people she had dismissed, that at some point she may have to experience this same unveiling toward everyone, toward the world at large. It was too much to consider at once and she allowed herself to remain only in the immediate disaster of the present.

He listened as she described the way that her mind had split neatly in two between what actually was, and what she was capable of tolerating, and how the false part had taken over and dominated the other for those months. There were details he didn't understand, logistics, about how she could take steps to hide her body from others to conceal the situation while also not actually acknowledging the situation to herself. She tried to explain how it went, how the threads of her mind had come loose and knotted together in nonsensical new iterations, so that when she tied a belt around her stomach or wore a big loose dress, her mind was only taking actions to make an appearance accord with the actual reality, which was that she was not pregnant.

It felt exhilarating to say these things to him, to a stranger, these things she had only spoken before in the vaguest of terms, to her mother who was now not alive to confirm that they had happened. She couldn't quite bring herself to speak about Lucy yet, about how it all connected and the appalling moment of suddenly comprehending the network of absences and silences she had facilitated which had led to this point.

She drank slowly, steadily, as they talked it over, and she unravelled in a way which appeared neither good nor bad but certainly transformative. They were sitting a foot apart at the desk with their chairs turned inward, very close, talking quietly but not looking at one another. It reminded Tom of exciting encounters at university when he would go back to a girl's room and listen to music and talk about books for hours with incredible earnestness, turning slowly toward each other throughout, until finally there was a natural lull in the rhythm of speech which was then taken up by sex.

His heart fluttered at the thought. He knew plenty who had done much worse; it was practically standard business to approach a call girl who had serviced a celebrity by having her yourself first and then revealing afterwards who you were and what you were after, for instance, and he knew that Brian Rylance who had since been moved to sport once called round to the house of the half-deranged mother of a stabbed teenager and slept with her before making her aware her son had died. It wouldn't be of that scale if he was to do something with Carmel, who was troubled but coherent and sane. To stop himself thinking about it he reached out and took her hand so that some action had been taken but one which could be walked back if necessary.

Why do you think you had to deny it so badly? he asked her. Was it just that getting rid of it wasn't an option over there?

It was partly that, Carmel said, but it was also that I thought I was special. Back then I thought I was really special, and destined for special things, and being pregnant was – felt like – oh God! – being pregnant felt like the least special, most ordinary and pathetic thing you could be. Never mind pregnant and not wanting it which was even more ugly and ordinary again. It's this big cloud that hangs over everyone in school, if you see what I mean, it's this misery hanging over whatever you do with boys, but it's also the only source of excitement and drama for these boring, stupid people who I hated, who I thought I was better than. It was a problem for another sort of girl, I wanted to be, I thought I was another sort of girl. Yes, a special one.

But you are special, aren't you? he said and touched her face and then her hair and then kissed her and she bent into him with relief and pressed her chapped hot mouth against him for a moment.

3.

They would speak about it amongst themselves after the boy had left the station, how brave and decent he had been despite his obvious terror and guilt, not to mention the poor parents who had to bring him in alongside everything else they were dealing with. Elliott Enright, brother of Mia, had come to share some further information he had not volunteered before. He had not lied, had not misled anyone

180

intentionally, but he was so appalled by the prospect of his own culpability that he hadn't been able to tell it all at once. It was true what he had told them, that he had last seen Mia with Lucy Green, but he had left out that he had seen the two of them and other children playing a certain kind of game together before he noticed she was missing.

He was only half paying attention, this was part of the problem, part of why he was torturing himself and didn't say it in the first instance. He was supposed to be looking after her but he was speaking to some new friends his own age. Mia was happy and occupied with the littler ones, so he wasn't fully cognisant of the situation. He was aware, though, that they were playing a game they called Freak Show: it was just a stupid one that those smaller kids did in school sometimes where they'd all show off funny or strange things they could do, like double-jointed digits, or rolling their tongues to look like a clover. He remembered that Lucy's trick was that she held her breath for so long, holding her nose theatrically and miming strangling herself, that her face turned an alarming bluish-purple, before she would let it all out in an ecstatic gust, the white rushing back to where it should be and her laughing too loudly, too shrilly.

He remembered seeing Lucy and an interchangeable half-dozen other kids playing this stupid game with each other, and Mia being among them and at one point he thought he had seen somebody holding Mia's nose and her sputtering and the rest of them laughing. He should have stopped it, but they weren't hurting her, she was laughing too, it was all a game, and she was so little, nobody would hurt her on purpose. The officers taking his statement would think often of the sound of his voice reaching its anguished pitch as he finished, face wrenched into a dreadful adult expression of self-loathing and defeat.

Elliott was the fourth child brought into the station that

day by parents who had been concerned by their reports of this game played with Mia. Their stories all broadly aligned – they had been playing it, and had wandered off one by one, leaving Mia and Lucy the last ones still at it, but at some point they had all been covering each other's mouths, holding the air inside their chests too long, looking at each another in the eye with trusting, thrilled fear.

They would soon have to release or charge Lucy Green for the crime of murdering Mia Enright, and with the new context of this game it was decided that she was to be released under investigation. It was acknowledged internally that she would not be arrested again, although it seemed likely it was Lucy who in the end killed Mia. It was no longer clear whether the killing was accidental or otherwise, and the corroboration of so many other children that a dangerous game was involved changed the texture of the incident. It was diffused now with enough doubt and disparate blame to mean something other than it had seemed at first. There would be social workers and extensive follow-up with the Green family, who would be advised that they should find alternative accommodation to Skyler Square as a matter of urgency, but there would be no criminal charge.

As it was late and Lucy had that evening been moved to a nearby foster-carer's home and was already sleeping, they decided they would wait until the morning to contact her mother to let her know what the outcome was and that she could now collect her child whenever she desired.

4.

They kissed for a moment, and she felt glad to have the feeling of novelty upon her. She had kissed three men since she had lived in London, two colleagues from the shop and an older man on the estate who didn't live there and was drunk in the stairwell one late night, drunk but debonair and wearing a cologne that smelled of seaweed and wood. It was a warm relief to kiss Tom, who was handsome and her own age and then she remembered why he was there, and broke away.

You can't write that in your stories because it would make you look as bad as me, she said.

Absolutely, he smiled, and took out a cigarette and lit it, and handed it to her, and then one for himself.

He asked her to say more about how she felt about the pregnancy, about being special. She made an embarrassed growl with half a laugh in it, and continued. The man who I was with, who was Lucy's father, he always made sure I knew I was special. He would always tell me that.

Tom thought to himself with excitement, wasn't that what they always said, girls who had been abused and taken advantage of, that their abusers made them feel special. Who was it, he practically cooed, leaning in toward her again, who was it who told you you were special?

Oh, God, it really doesn't matter, honestly, she said and took another drink of the wine, running her tongue over her teeth because they felt squalid and mossy now.

Who was it, Carmel? he asked, taking her hand. You can tell me. I will understand, I swear I will. I won't judge you.

I don't know what you mean, she said, not removing her hand, but frowning at him in frank confusion.

He cradled her face in his hand and said, You can tell me.

Possibilities were thrumming through his exhausted brain. He felt that this was his moment to get something real, while she was soft and open and confused, and yet he still did not know what the real something was, what it was he had to uncover. The vague darknesses revealed to him by each member of the family held no narrative coherence when placed together, he could not get a grip on them.

Richie's despair, his lack of memory, seemed in the urgency of the moment the most suggestive to probe. Where there was absence, there could be anything at all to replace it. What Richie was failing to remember could be any number of things, things which would be good enough for a proper story.

Richie told me he was supposed to look after Lucy the afternoon when it all happened, when Mia went missing, Tom said.

Yes, so? He was often supposed to look after her.

Yes exactly, exactly, Tom said, he was often supposed to look after her but he can't remember what happens in those hours. He's missing a lot of time.

I don't know what you're getting at, said Carmel, becoming annoyed now. I know Richie's an alcoholic. Everyone who's ever met Richie since he was fifteen knows he's an alcoholic. What's the surprise that he can't remember things?

It's a very interesting thing to say – to confess actually, is how I'd put it – in the aftermath of a child being killed. That you can't remember the time in question, Tom said. He felt hot, happily anxious, as though he was getting somewhere interesting. If I were being questioned I'd be frightened to say I couldn't remember where I was at the time of an awful crime – I'd be frightened because of how guilty and suspicious that would make me sound.

Richie wasn't being questioned, because you're not a policeman, said Carmel, you're a con man who was giving him enough booze to make him think you're his friend.

But Tom was talking over her, determined to rattle something out now.

If he can't remember where he was, if he only came to hours later by which time Lucy was in bed, how do we know Richie didn't have something to do with it too? These things happen you know, families, bad influences. There was a killer in America who inducted his son into the whole business with him, terrible thing—

Tom squirmed in his chair, getting breathless, grinning pathetically at her.

Nobody will blame Lucy, if that's how it was, he said. Lucy killed Mia. She did it, we all know that. But we can tell your story and explain why she did it. If Richie were a part of it somehow, if Richie was the one really responsible for Mia, or if he did something awful to Lucy. Or to you! I'm not the monster here, Carmel, I know that children aren't just born like that, they aren't just born evil—

She swung at him, she got a good go at him. She would find his fine soft skin underneath her nails the next day.

5.

Carmel's arms shook with anger and fright. She circled around the drawing room looking for something to focus them on. There was a set of crystal decanters on a desk, full of nothing, which she took the lids off one by one. Then she opened the cupboard drawer beside the desk which had a Bible and a phone directory inside, both of which she grabbed out and threw disconsolately on the floor.

Imagine him saying that, she kept repeating to her father, without actually telling him what Tom had alleged, unable to voice something so incoherent and bizarre. John was now mostly sober after his sleep, and trying to take in what his daughter was saying, but she was bouncing from one part to another without segue.

And Lucy didn't mean to do anything to anyone, she shouted, whatever happened – and we don't even know yet what happened! – she gasped, she didn't mean to do it. How could she mean to do anything, when she's barely a baby herself, she's barely fucking alive herself?

She stood there in the middle of the room, angry at its shitty faded grandeur, thin arms wrapped so far on either side of her head that they jutted out and made her look alien and unreal, covering her, blocking out sound.

Her whole body was shaking, a green knit cardigan she had taken from Richie's room as he slept vibrating around her.

She didn't do it, she didn't do it, she didn't do it, she was saying, hands clasped over her ears, eyes shut.

When she felt on the ground that her father had stood up from the bed and was coming near to her she made an ugly face and clasped them tighter and said I can't, I can't, I can't.

John walked to her, and put his hands over hers, where they clung to the sides of her skull. For a minute he let them rest there as she repeated it. He laid his over hers and they were so total and so warm and she had forgotten all about them and their power. The mere fact that they were so much bigger than her own, and what that had meant when she was little, what their comparative largeness gave her. He stood like that with her for minutes as they both let her work herself into a certain limited pitch and then agreed without words that it was enough.

He took her hands and put them on her own heart. He pressed them tight against it with one hand. He used his other hand to take her chin and bring it gently upward an inch from where it was, so that she was looking him in the eye.

I need you to listen to me now, Carmel, he said, and I know you have every reason to have not listened to me for years, and other reasons to have never listened to me a day in your life. But now I need you to listen. I didn't need you to listen any other time before, I didn't have anything to say.

She wasn't able to meet his eye yet but her face was level with his and she had grabbed on to his hand on hers, over her heart.

Lucy did kill that baby, he said, and her eyes flew even further up than they had been before, were fluttering now somewhere inside her skull, outside of space, and she was letting out a terrible low growling sound which dimly recalled the sound of a cat he had once had to kill because of its stomach being distended with cancer or some other evil. A totally new sound, from an underground place.

Lucy did kill that baby, he said again, grabbing her chin more firmly now and trying to get her to look at him, we know it, there's no denying it – I knew as soon as they came to take her that she did it, from the way she acted. She might not have meant to do it, but she did. And that will never, ever be any different than it is. I'm not trying to be cruel to you, Carmel. I swear to God and on your mother and my own mother, if there was a way I could lie to you about this I would lie until the day I died. But I can't do that, and the best I can do for you instead is to make you believe it now so that you don't go mad.

Carmel's body was extended as far upward as it could possibly go, up on her tiptoes, reaching up to the end of things, the top of the sky where it went dark. She strained out of her father's hands as he spoke, but when he said the word 'mad' she couldn't bear it and softened back down into the room. When she did so she felt his hands on her and was disgusted, throwing him off and shaking her arms as though she'd been soaked in something unbearable.

Don't touch me, she wept, hugging her arms around herself and shrinking from him. She sat down at the desk.

I wish I could leave you alone, he said, but we have to talk to one another now to make sure that you don't go mad, and that Lucy doesn't go mad either.

And she could tell even through her terrific fright that this was the only true and useful thing her father had said in twenty years.

6.

Still seething, Tom lay on the bed with his hands pressed down on his chest trying to regulate his erratic racing heart. He thought miserably of Richie's grab-bag of assorted physical ailments to which he had eagerly referred earlier, and wondered which of them he would be developing over the next few years if he kept drinking like this. It was unbelievable, unthinkable, that he had had them here for twenty-four hours and had gotten nothing. When he closed his eyes he saw Carmel's eyes flash with hatred and anger but he refused to be cowed by it, responded to it with his own, feeling derision for the thick-headed loyalty her silence indicated. If she had agreed to work with him, it really might have turned out alright for her, or better than it would now in any case. Now, her life was over, simple as that. Thinking of her mournful mouth on his, he flipped over so that he was face down and masturbated vengefully into the decaying duvet before drifting into restless sleep.

It was in this position he was woken by the phone ringing a few hours later, at 6 a.m. When he stumbled over to answer it and heard Edward's unfeasibly chipper tone he felt extremely aware of the clamminess of the hand holding the receiver, and the feeling of thirty drinks and twice as many cigarettes in his mouth and chest.

You sound well, Edward laughed, and it was amazing how he was as buoyant and casual and keen as he always was.

Ha, ha! Tom coughed back at him, and having cleared his throat asked why he was calling.

Bit of an unfortunate one for us, I'm afraid, Tom. I've just had a call from one of our inside blokes at the station and they're releasing that little Irish thing who's been causing you so much trouble.

What do you mean, releasing her?

It's all done now, more or less. There'll be a formal investigation to say so, but it seems it was actually a bit of a game, an accident, death by misadventure if that isn't too morbid to say it that way.

So that's it, Tom asked incredulously, they let her go and nothing happens to her? None of this goes anywhere?

Yes, that's what I'm telling you – you are hungover, aren't you? I mean at the end of the day she's a little kid so if it was an accident they aren't going to want to do a show trial and throw away the key, are they? And nor would we frankly, doesn't sit right unless it's totally clear-cut. Did you get anything intriguing from the family anyway, out of interest?

Yes, Tom said, there was a lot of it.

Ah, shame. I know this is a disappointment and it would have been a big one for you, but it happens to the best of us. There'll be plenty more. Have a bit more kip and come in for ten, will you, there's something I want you on. Oh, and send word to that freelance fellow's hotel in Ireland that he can abscond.

Edward hung up.

Tom stood trembling before the window taking it in, how casually Edward had spoken of the evaporation, how little it had meant to him, how it would all mean absolutely nothing to anyone now. Nobody would ever think of this again except for the children who had played that game and the dead child's grieving family. Them, and the family he had spent two nights and a day with, and an unknowable child of theirs who would be free in the morning. None of it meant anything, and this knowledge filled him with such rage that he felt it rush toward Lucy for some reason, who had not played her part sufficiently, not definitively enough, but whose actions had nonetheless reduced him.

189

She had compelled his casual barbarism to her family, to wish that a child murdered another child. Maybe it was true and maybe it wasn't, but he had wished for its truth anyway and he would always know that about himself now. It would not even be possible to justify it by thinking, by saying, but hey, what a story, what a scoop, what an amazing sleight of hand.

7.

Richie slept deeply that night, and in the further part of his dreams there was a small and humble piazza where he took charge and he handed out moderately measured glasses of delicious things to people who needed them in only the right amount.

8.

Carmel had slept in her father's big bed, too frightened to be by herself. At one point, in his sleep, he reached over and held the back of her skull in his hand and gently squeezed it, and then said aloud from his sleep, Oh, four times, faintly: Oh, oh, oh, oh.

She thought, I missed you – God, how I missed you, but then tears filled her eyes as she thought that he had never been there to miss. She knew that this brief intimacy was finite, like the sound you hear ringing in your ear to signify that damage has killed that particular pitch there, and it will never be heard again.

The phone rang at seven, and a family-liaison officer told Carmel that Lucy wasn't being charged, but would likely be called back in for further questions as part of the investigation.

Carmel was unable to speak coherently to the woman, and handed the phone to her father for a moment while she stood with her hand pressed to her mouth and looked towards him, pleading. He spoke to her for a few minutes and noted down an address where they were to go and collect the child.

Don't forget what I said, please, John said to Carmel when he had hung up. She can't be allowed to pretend this didn't happen.

Carmel nodded fervently, not knowing exactly what this would mean in practice, but knowing there was something crucial in his impulse, some gift of experience he needed to bestow.

She put her hand on his and they sat on the bed together for a time, not wanting their closeness to end but waiting for it to, thinking about what would happen next.

9.

At 8.30 a.m. all the members of the Green family had left the hotel and were standing out in the courtyard, waiting for a taxi which would take them to where Lucy was. The light poured down on them and Richie and Carmel turned their faces toward it, as though they were vampires, as though they had been in the hotel for years and years.

Tom Hargreaves left his room a few minutes later than they did, and loitered in the porch, badly afraid. He was afraid to think of what he had done the day before, he was afraid of these people he had done it to, but after the taxi didn't come for twenty minutes, he walked carefully over to Carmel, aware that Richie and John were looking on. He took her gently by the elbow and she instantly jerked it away.

How dare you touch me, she said, but it was without heart; she wasn't angry with him now that they were going to get Lucy, only exhausted.

I'm sorry, he said.

What for?

I'm sorry I assumed things, tried to bully things out of you.

Yeah, well – you're a fool, anyway, barking up that tree, Carmel said, turning away.

Wait, Tom said, now that it doesn't matter any more – can you tell me?

Tell you what? she asked.

Can you tell me what the secret really is, what you've all been keeping from me?

She stood back a moment and looked at him, only a boy, a stupid boy, just another boy trying to do something he didn't understand and would never feel the consequences of. She envied him. There was a time when she thought her life would be something like his, being out in the world affecting things, doing things to people and being light and nimble and special enough not to have to deal with their reactions. Even being near his cool breezy charm the evening before, in the midst of her worst misery, had felt refreshing. An enlivening reminder of other sorts of lives, that she might have one. She would never admit as much to anyone for the rest of her life but there had passed a moment in that room when she had imagined Lucy would get taken away and it would be possible for her to finally fully forget, move on, excise.

She leaned in close to him, pressing her nose into his clean fragrant hair and neck, letting herself enjoy it once more. There is no secret, Tom, or else there are hundreds of them, and none of them interesting enough for you. The secret is that we're a family, we're just an ordinary family, with ordinary unhappiness like yours.

10.
Waterford

The freelance reporter, an amiable middle-aged man named Robert, was contacted and called off by Tom before he had even had time to eat breakfast. With the B&B paid for and nothing pressing to return to, he decided to stay for the day regardless. He asked the landlady if there were anything in particular he should visit, and she directed him to a Viking tower which, when he saw it, would surprise him by being roughly the height of the houses in Primrose Hill despite its name.

It's a beautiful day, she said as she sent him off.

It is, he agreed.

Well, we'll pay for that tomorrow, the woman tutted and Robert thought with amusement how much the Irish were still like pagans or spiritualists, always offering sacrifices to restore balance, and the balance was usually being drawn down into the negative quarter.

He walked through the People's Park and up Catherine Street and then through the narrow Lady Lane into the Apple Market, where he saw a smart-looking Italian cafe and thought he would have something to eat. A good-looking, friendly woman with silver threaded prettily through her dark hair greeted him and poured his water and told him the specials, mussels in parmesan cream, octopus with toasted almonds and red pepper sauce, he was impressed and mildly, patronisingly surprised, and she asked what he was up to in Waterford.

I was supposed to be here reporting a story, he told her, but it's been cancelled now, so I'll just have a look round and an early night and head back on a flight in the morning.

A newspaper story? I can't believe there's anything

interesting enough happening around here to bring you all this way, she said.

It was something that happened in England, actually, but the family involved used to live here, they moved over years ago. Anyway the story hasn't turned out to be anything now, that's how it goes sometimes.

Bella went into the kitchen to see the chef, Luke, who had also become her husband, and said to him, I think Richie Green may have come to something bad.

That was always going to be the way, Luke said.

Was it, she wondered, and reproached herself as she sometimes did for not offering to give him a second chance. She had seen him once, three years before, in London for the weekend on her hen party. He was walking toward the pub that she and her friends were sat outside, and he had retained the basic shape and sense of himself, the similar clothes and build, but within the borders everything was muddled and distended. He was swaying lightly as he walked, holding a beer, and she thought he had stopped looking specific and now looked like any number of winos you would see without fully taking them in. He passed by and it was too small a space between them to believe he didn't see her too, but neither of them spoke.

11.
LUCY
London

She had slept well that night, in the strange but plush bedroom filled with teddy bears, checked on by the stern, kind woman who looked a bit like Rose if Rose were bigger and taller and hadn't died, had been allowed to get as old. In the morning she watched from the window as the carer, protective already of her brief charge, had waited outside to meet Carmel and Richie and John, wanting to create a barrier between Lucy and her family. She watched as her mother climbed out of a taxi, agonisingly beautiful, followed by an official-looking lady who spoke to the carer and Carmel together for several minutes, explaining how the next few weeks would go.

Lucy waited until the carer came to get her and held her hand as she went down the stairs, suddenly afraid, lingering back in the door frame, seeing her grandfather and Richie waving from inside the taxi. She felt heavy with dread at the thought of going back to Skyler Square and seeing the other children and the flat. She felt shy too because her mother was looking at her with a novel focus, peering analytically as though trying to add Lucy's parts to see what they made up, and although she had longed for her mother's focus it was painful too.

Carmel walked towards her and everything felt awkward and shocking, as though they had been separated for a much longer time than they had. She wondered what sort of trouble she would now be in and how long it would go on for. This was one thing she missed often about Rose, that she would always give the times for things without Lucy having to ask; she would say how long until dinner would be ready, and how much longer until the summer holidays, and the time they would be finished having a bath. Without her, nobody gave time any structure so that bad days or delayed meals seemed like they might well go on forever, there was no way to know.

Her mother crouched down now, and seemed to want to do something but was unsure exactly what it was. She moved as though to touch Lucy and Lucy flinched: although she had never hit her she had also touched her so rarely that it was alarming. So Carmel stopped moving and folded her arms to keep them from their restlessness, and

195

instead only looked Lucy in the eye and said the beginning of what the following years would be occupied with trying to say and show, she said I'm sorry, I'm sorry, I'm so so sorry. And then she said, let's go home, and did not mean Skyler Square.

Part VIII

1.
Home
September 1990

Carmel had a desperate, inordinate terror of haunted houses all her life. It was a source of mockery for Richie and their cousins growing up, out at the amusements in Tramore next to the sea, that she would descend immediately into extreme hysterics as soon as the doors of the ghost train creaked open and the wagon pushed through. It didn't matter that it was so amateur and slapdash, nor how many times she was forced to go through it. Seeing the same tricks pop out from the familiar corners, the witch's face crashing down into her own, the moaning man in face paint who clawed after her as they turned a bend. There was no amount that she could memorise the way it would all take place which lessened the terror.

She sporadically assumed it must have only been her youth which had caused this reaction – naturally she was frightened at ten but it could be handled at the more sophisticated age of eleven – and would insist on trying again. Every year it happened again, the horror so out-sized as to appear obviously false and attention seeking, her screaming help me, help me, please help me and clutching Richie with such force she left bruises, but each time was completely authentic. Eventually she realised she would never out-think whatever it was she couldn't tolerate in the haunted house.

When they returned to Waterford, there was a part of her which thought that the house in Mayor's Walk would feel this way. She feared it would reveal its past darkness ceaselessly, no matter how familiar and worn the territory was, and each time she crossed a threshold there would be some ghastly oppressive presence waiting to disarm her. When she and Lucy and John arrived to it, the superstitious side of her noted the cobwebs growing over the hinge of the front door in their picturesque forbiddance, but took it as a good sign that John swiftly wiped them away muttering about slatternly tenants.

She had been wrong about Mayor's Walk being haunted. It felt more like a doll's house which had been made liveable, astonishing to walk through so quickly and easily. The quiet and space of the vacated rooms helped to neutralise it. Only in the window frames could she feel the reverberations of the threatening melancholy she feared. How small the windows were, and how much portent and yearning she could remember focusing out of them; into the world, toward Derek and another way of living. They had felt large enough to escape through then.

She took Lucy by the hand to tour her through it, slowly and gently as she had learned to touch her child – neither brisk and harsh as she once had been, nor overbearing and needy as she sometimes was inclined to be after all that had happened. Carmel tried not to expect anything at all from her yet, and tried not to wonder how what had taken place in Skyler Square would shape the future. There had been something useful in the administration, the immediate requirements of the move back to Ireland. They made her feel practical and responsible, of use, made her feel like Rose.

Rose was here in the house, in Mayor's Walk. She felt that

presence in its forgiveness, its lack of fright. There was a great swelling of love and pleasure in her throat as she understood this. It wasn't that she believed in ghosts, she thought, she never had, not even on the ghost train in Tramore, but there was something tangible in certain rooms. You could feel it even in the Hotel Gargano on those awful nights, the layers of sadness and short-lived ecstasies accumulating for decades. And here there was the inarguable sense of Rose, in her old bedroom, in the kitchen where she sat with her friends and laughed and was young and well.

It was the last place that Rose existed as her old self, and as a healthy person, it was the last place she resided in which she was only alive, never dying. There was a way here in which Carmel could suspend reality and summon the feeling that Rose was not dead but elsewhere – a place you could not return from but which was less resolved and less unacceptable than the truth. She had promised to stop denying the truth, to strive always to confront things as they were no matter how much it hurt, but she felt that this was one area an exception could be made. To stand in these rooms and believe however briefly that death was a thing which happened only in a foreign country, and could not follow you home.

Of all the rooms, she was most afraid to go in her own. It was the one she had sometimes shared with Richie but had endured her worst suffering in entirely alone. The airless quality of those months when her mind split apart from her body was still too vivid. To think of it, how she scoured and beat and hurt herself, was so shameful and ugly. Walking with Lucy into the narrow single room, dusty in the sunlight, it was amazing that so little space could have held that sort of boundless morphing pain.

While Carmel surveyed from the door frame, Lucy ambled ahead and hopped up to sit on the window ledge and look out onto the street she would live the rest of her childhood in. Her small solid presence appeared as a vindication, in that moment at least. Remarkable for her to be breathing and humming and thinking, even now, even as her thoughts remained mysterious and frightening to Carmel. It was amazing any of her existed at all, after the violence in this same room she now occupied. She felt something like fondness or a grudging admiration, not toward her daughter but toward life itself, how persistent and absurd and reckless a force it could be.

2.

In December, when Lucy had been in school at the Ursuline convent for almost three months, her teacher sent a note home asking Carmel to come in on Thursday after lessons had ended. The teacher, a nun named Sister Pauline who had in decades past taught both Carmel and Rose, was ancient in the smooth timeless way of certain holy people. It wasn't a scheduled parent evening, so it was clear to Carmel that something was wrong. As she got ready to leave, it became increasingly evident that she was terrified of what would be told to her now. She was aware of her stomach muscles clenching in pre-emptive defence and the familiar metallic tang watering in the back of her throat, body getting ready to panic or shut down.

What are you afraid of? she asked herself, looking at Lucy who was sitting on the couch with her grandfather watching *Art Attack* and forming a necklace from sopping papier mâché. He was looking after her while the meeting went on, as he did on evenings Carmel worked in the pub on O'Connell Street, and the rare times she would go to the cinema. John looking after Lucy meant something very different than it once had, before what had happened in Skyler

Square. It didn't mean just to be in the same house as her. He and Carmel had discussed this, how they must keep her busy, as they never did before. He made small things with her, taught her to play card games, read books together. Even if there was still an unreachable reserve in him, he made himself available and useful in this way.

Great haunting gaps in Lucy's childhood surfaced in Carmel's mind now, vacant timeframes she hadn't noticed as they occurred. The many afternoons and evenings in the years following Rose's death when Lucy was alive but unknown, alone and folded into small corners of the flat, or existing ambiently in the hallways and porches of the estate. It sickened Carmel to think of the unaccounted hours, not only because of guilt but from fear of the thoughts and feelings which may have grown inside the child, silent and spore-like, in all that solitude.

What are you afraid of? she asked herself, and had to answer that she was afraid of Sister Pauline revealing a sign, however subtle, that those hours had ruined Lucy forever, that what she did to Mia wasn't a terrible accident, a game gone wrong. She was afraid it was just the beginning. She was afraid that Lucy had hurt someone else, that perhaps Lucy would never stop hurting other people, even if she wanted to. The question of wanting was another there was no answer to; whether she had killed out of desire, or compulsion, or purely through bad luck and a child's ill conception of physical reality and the permanence of death.

Once, very soon after returning to Ireland, Carmel had tried to ask the question.

Did you mean to do it? To Mia? she asked as she put her to bed that night. The question wasn't planned, it tumbled out of her, and she clasped a hand over her mouth after the words emerged. Lucy had gone rigid and jerked toward the wall, pressing herself firmly against it forehead first, her face slackening and emptying out. Carmel sat with her for a

203

long time, holding one hand firmly to her back, touching her hair, in case she began to speak, but nothing came except quick breaths. At last she had pulled the blankets around her fully and turned out the light and left the room. She stood outside in the hall, thinking that she must find somebody who could help Lucy speak, thinking that she had no idea how to do this or how to find the money to achieve it. Then she thought of the horror of being stuck in the dark alone with that question for the whole endless night, and slipped back into her daughter's bedroom and sat on the chair listening until she heard her breaths slow and pacify into sleep.

Waterford had, on the whole, been less charged and unsettling to return to than Carmel had assumed it would be, but this did not hold true in her old school. Walking up the slight incline towards its entrance she felt an echo of the uncomplicated hope she had once begun each day with as a child, charging up this path toward her friends and the golden future. To walk there now, it was impossible not to feel that the impulse could somehow still realise itself, that she could step back into that time and correct its course. Then she thought of how Lucy had not felt that way in her life, how none of her childhood had been pristine or hopeful.

Carmel had dwelled so long in the characteristic tragedy of her own childhood, and had forgotten to be grateful that, before it, hers was an essentially good life. It was imperfect but sturdy, with the baseline of oblivious optimism born of parental love. For all that had gone wrong, there were lessons and inclinations buried beneath the years of dissolution.

Lucy didn't have that, she reminded herself. If Sister Pauline does say she has hurt some other child, remember that Lucy didn't have that, and stay with her, help her again, as many times as it takes. It is the least you can do, all you can do.

Inside, the classrooms smelled as she remembered them – as the police station had – of fresh paint and radiators. Sister Pauline invited her to sit down and asked after her family. Carmel was unsure what exactly was known in the community about London, but even the original sin of having had Lucy at all, as an unwed teenager, was enough to make her guilty. It seemed always as though clergy and nuns knew everything about her before she spoke, a suspicion confirmed as a child when she had gone to make her first confession but had no sins to confess. She had fabricated a few to fill the time, saying she fought with her brother, and stole a bar of chocolate, and the priest had paused ominously before saying, Do you know that telling priests lies is one of the biggest sins?

Lucy isn't in trouble, Sister Pauline said, seeing Carmel's worry, But she isn't doing well. I don't know what the precise circumstances were that brought you home—

Carmel began to speak but the nun raised her hand to stop her.

I don't need to know them, but Lucy is not settling in here.

Is she misbehaving?

Not exactly, no, but her behaviour makes it impossible to function in the school appropriately. She's behind in her lessons by a long way, but I'm not overly concerned about that. She's bright enough and if she needs to stay back a year that won't be the end of the world. The problem is she won't talk to the other children.

Confused, Carmel asked, You mean she can't make any friends? It will probably just take a while for the other children to get used to her, won't it?

No, it's the other way. The other girls were interested in her, they did wish to befriend her. She's very pretty, of course, and they were intrigued by her accent. Quite a few of them went out of their way to include her, but she ignored them, wouldn't respond at all. Ultimately it isn't my business who Lucy wants to spend time with on a social basis, but it is so extreme that it's disrupting lessons now. Say if they have to swap tests to correct the other's, she won't speak to the girl. She'll take it from me if I come over and tell her directly, but never acknowledges the other child. In PE yesterday she was told to join up with another girl to help each other do tumbles and cartwheels and when the girl sat down on the mat with her and touched her she burst into tears. We have tried to be gentle and encourage her but it's getting to a point where she can't participate at all. Can you shed any light on this, Carmel, or help us to help her?

Carmel looked down at her hands which were clasped prayer-like and, not knowing where to begin, wept.

3.
1994

Lucy had been seeing Miss Nealon – Diane, after they spent some time together – for a year before she told her about the dreams. Miss Nealon was young and appealing and at first Lucy could not bear to meet her eyes as they spoke. Sessions passed at arduous length, Lucy's inability to make small talk exacerbated by the box of tissues and the cloying suggestion of emotion which saturated the room. Muted floral decor gave it the tone of an institution or a funeral parlour. She was astonished the day she realised Diane lived in the same house as the office.

Don't you mind living above all this? she asked, waving her hand around the room indicating what she thought of as its permanent atmosphere of distress.

Diane laughed. No, she said, why would I? I help people here, to me it's a positive place.

But you must hear things, awful things? said Lucy, and

they were both quiet for a moment, reflecting on the fact that Lucy had never yet said aloud her awful things.

She reported the minutiae of family life with her mother and grandfather on a purely contemporary basis, never offering insight or context. She spoke of difficulty at school in the same monotone, boring and frustrating herself and, she suspected, Diane, who wished her to speak intimately.

She longed for Diane's approval but it was an unfulfillable desire, one she could only satisfy by revealing her monstrosity, which would then make Diane hate and fear her. That knowledge she kept safe in her centre, neutralised by many layers of cultivated stillness. She had learned that it was a better use of energy to suppress her urge toward restless movement – the fidgeting and repetitive jerks and self-injury – than to let it go untethered. Using the same force which drove it, she boiled the urge down to a tight hard gem inside herself. She could almost physically feel the force of effort crashing over it when it threatened to emerge. It was pleasing to think she had changed herself on purpose, that there was at least one item of proof of her ability to do so.

She was learning like her mother once had in the same bedroom in Mayor's Walk that reality was a malleable concept, that living with her private knowledge was bearable if her external affect betrayed no sign of it. If she behaved and appeared as though it didn't exist, then almost all of the time it really didn't exist. There were interims when nobody else was present during which it existed fully, these could not be avoided and had to simply be withstood. They passed.

Something about the new knowledge that Diane lived in such proximity to the place she saw her clients made Lucy feel restless.

I wouldn't have guessed you lived here, she said, it doesn't seem your style.

What do you think my style is? Diane asked.

I don't know, just you're young.

I'm not that young – I'm your mother's age. If we didn't go to different schools I think we would have been in the same class.

My mother is young too, Lucy said, shrugging.

Well, we're not here to talk about me but my mother wasn't young, she was a lot older than most of my friends' mothers, and she died a few years ago and left me this house. That's why it feels a bit old-fashioned, I haven't got round to decorating it yet.

Lucy thought for a moment. Did you know she was going to die? she asked.

Why do you ask?

I didn't know that Rose was going to die. Even when she died I didn't know she was dead.

Diane waited, and then asked, You didn't know what it meant to be dead, you mean?

Nobody told me, Lucy said. They didn't tell me she was going to die, and when she died they didn't tell me what that meant. It was like they all thought someone else had told me so they didn't bother doing it. How was I supposed to know? I didn't know anybody who died before that, and nobody spelled it out.

That's very upsetting. It must have made you feel very confused. How do you feel telling me about it now?

I'm angry, Lucy said, I'm angry all the time and I can't tell anyone that.

Why not?

Because of what I did. I'm afraid that if I'm angry with my mother then she'll remind me what I did, because it's so much worse than anything she did. So I can't be angry.

Do you want to talk about what you did?

No, Lucy said.

For the first few years after she had come to Ireland it was as though her mind had whitened with shock. There was nothing definitively real between the solid memory of the game in the courtyard – raucous laughter and plenty of other children around – and the solid memory of being in bed feeling sick and scared that night listening to her uncle Richie crash around in the sitting room talking to himself. What came in the middle had warped and become slippery, irretrievable. Lucy had already felt from her earliest childhood that her mind was fundamentally flawed and couldn't hold things the way that other people seemed to effortlessly, so the fluidity of the missing hours did not feel especially surprising. What was to be gained in their clarification? And yet sometimes the pictures did come. It was difficult for Lucy to know which dream to fear the most, the good one or the bad. In the good one, the one which felt euphoric as it took place but devastating to emerge from into waking life, there were flashes of the boy she had once hurt in the school playground. The scene was the same, her kneeling over an injured child, but the figure changed sometimes so that there was a flash of pink plastic from the glasses and pretty golden blondness. In the dream these flashes were innocently beautiful and pleasing, unlike in life. Lucy bent over the figure and lay with it and touched it gently and suddenly they were both warmed from within by a gentle pulsing light, health and peace rushing and joining them, colour flooding to the surface and a feeling of great calm and resolution.

I don't sleep well, she said to Diane.

Why not?

In the other sort of dream, that which came a dozen times a year, she was older than her true age. The setting varied in specific detail, but always she was in a house in which she had concealed a body. Now, people were coming to renovate the house and she knew that they would break down the wall, or prise up the floorboards, which had contained her secret. Sometimes it was a long-kept secret, she had hidden the body many years ago.

There was a vivid image of hacking at a flimsy wall and

releasing clouds of dry dust to make a space. In this scenario she had an accomplice, there was the feeling of a person lingering behind her who was even more frightened than she was, who she was trying to protect. Then the nauseating weight of a limp human being, pushing limbs, the body refusing to be corralled and falling back out on top of her. The sealing up of this tomb, and the feeling of decades, more, somehow being conveyed in the space of this one dream, the burden of always knowing for every second of that life that the body was there and could be found at any time. Finally the day arrived which she knew always must, that someone would uncover this most dreadful and truest part of herself, and she stood helpless in the house as they began their work. The surprising thing about the dream was that sometimes it ended with a surge of ecstatic relief, the only wish that it had happened long ago, that life had not been wasted waiting for this day.

Do you think of me differently now that I told you that? Lucy asked.

I think differently about you every time I learn something new about you, Diane said, but that doesn't mean I think worse of you. Do you feel different now that I know about the dreams?

Yes, said Lucy.

Well, Diane said to her, don't you want to feel different than you do?

4.
The Future
Waterford, 1996

Six years after Carmel and Lucy and John had moved back to Waterford and into Mayor's Walk, Carmel was walking through the park when she saw Derek O'Toole. He was

210

walking hand in hand with a small blonde woman, both of them cracking up.

She had seen him before he noticed her, and in the intervening moments she had an almighty urge to run over and tell him everything, absolutely all of it.

She would tell him about the pregnancy and the sort of mad she had gone – which she knew now other women had and did too, she was not the only person in the world whose mind had disjointed in that particular way, knowledge which would provide unexpectedly enormous relief. She would tell him about Lucy being born and how hard it was to look at her so that she just stopped instead and let Rose do it for her. She would tell him about Rose dying and how monstrously unfair it was, the way the prosaic natural tragedies of life kept happening even when the unexpected and unusual sort were taking place too. She would tell him, of course, about Lucy being detained and those strange days in the hotel, a time and place that felt so sodden with misery and darkness that she doubted she would ever be able to return to that part of London again if she ever went back at all, it had rendered it so infected and malign.

She would tell him about the strange hinterland months and the social-worker visits and the investigation concluding. She would tell him about returning to Ireland and how they pleaded with Richie to come back home with them but he had resisted, saying that it didn't matter where he went, he had learned that from the first time he had fled and tried to start all over. And then the haunted weeks she and Lucy and her father had spent in his mother's dilapidated cottage near the sea, waiting until the tenants in Mayor's Walk were leaving, how the three of them had to try to get to know one another again and how it was agonising and awkward and she often wanted to give up and run away, but sometimes it began to work and the feeling of being a family, which she had not felt since she was a child, came back.

She wanted to say it all to him, not to punish him, but because in this new part of her life she had become fixated on truth and confrontation. Her father's advice in the hotel had ended up giving her the zeal of the convert and she was somewhat manic with it. Her instinct was to say everything, no matter what it was, to leave no possible opening for the sort of secret keeping which had taken place, the kind that burrowed down into your stomach and changed who you were and made you sick. She had pushed her father to take his own word and be actively forthcoming and exlporatory with his past and his current emotions, but as she had intuited that night, he had been pushed toward change only by the extreme pressure of crisis. His ancient habits were easy to return to, especially back in Waterford, where he was more contented than in England but much the same removed presence she had grown up with. She was trying to accept that she couldn't force her reactive honesty on others, couldn't speak into their silences for them.

Nor, she thought, would it do anyone any good to produce all of her sadness for Derek now, or to ask things of him when it was too late, when it would only have done anyone any good if she had spoken at the time. She would discuss it with Lucy, and if she wanted to make contact with him then they would think it through together. When Derek clocked her he didn't appear surprised despite the half a lifetime which had elapsed between when they had last seen one another and the present, only broke instantly into his old familiar grin. He introduced his wife as Lottie, and she smiled at Carmel too, and she thought what a strikingly beautiful couple they were.

Carmel used to come in and cry at the pictures once a week when I worked there, he told Lottie, laughing.

When he asked how she was and she mentioned her daughter Lucy he simply congratulated her with easy warmth. It was astonishing to see how none of it caused him any curiosity or discomfort – for him, she really had just been the funny girl who cried in the pictures who he went out with for a few months before his real life began. She could scarcely remember, let alone empathise with, her reasoning at the time for not letting herself tell him what had happened, what they had done together. Pride, she supposed, that was all, but this was such a deranged cause and such a foreign feeling to her now that it was difficult to credit. They said goodbye to one another with the usual vague intention to see one another properly at some undefined future time.

Carmel walked thoughtfully up to the house, where she would wait for Lucy to get home from school. They lived together in the tidy, small space which had hosted so many of their family's defining misfortunes but which nonetheless felt sturdy and safe. John had died a year before of a heart attack in his sleep. This was said to be the most civilised way to die, feeling nothing, expecting nothing, but its suddenness was its own affront, particularly for Carmel who felt their limited attempts to speak and live openly with one another had only just begun to bear fruit – he would make eye contact without you having to search it out of him, and didn't read at the dinner table every night, sometimes even let the dishes sit on the table a while as they chatted about their days.

Since he had been gone the house felt calmer still, only the two of them, both neat and careful of the other. Lucy remained smaller than average and sometimes Carmel felt harrowing shame when she looked at her tiny shoes, thinking of those months pushing her down and trying to make her disappear. She was gorgeous now, much like her mother had been and often was. They tried their hardest with one another, which is not to say they always did well. At the beginning Carmel had felt it was a problem with a solution, that the absence of her affection and attention had been the issue, and that she needed only to urgently push those things onto Lucy for her to be better and for them to be happy. She knew now that it didn't work that way, that the things you did or failed to do could not be erased by anything, not even love.

But still, they tried. The trying would be the life's work, they both understood this, and there would be no day when they would celebrate a resolution.

A sort of ritual was established, once or twice a year, in which they would sit down together and speak about what happened with Mia. Lucy would try her best to say what she remembered and how she felt, what she could stand to think about and what she wasn't able to picture or describe. The process became harder the older she grew, the further she travelled from that moment, a moment which Carmel was barely any closer to truly imagining than she had been at the time. The facts grew fuzzy, and Lucy, becoming a teenager, began naturally to resist being forced to sit and confront her gravest trauma with her mother – after all, a teenage girl can loathe and disrespect her mother for far less serious sins than those Carmel had committed. But still, they tried.

In a more straightforward ritual, they took out photographs of Rose and looked at them together and spoke about their favourite times with her. Lucy liked to hear about their family as it had existed before her conception, and there was part of Carmel which wanted to assure her that things weren't perfect even then, that Lucy wasn't the force which caused so much unhappiness – but there were things she remembered, moments that could barely even be called memories they were of so little consequence, the feeling of biting down into a butter and sugar sandwich at the beach and not knowing immediately if the crunch was sand or grains of sweetness which reminded her that, yes, it had been good, yes, they were a family, and sometimes a very happy one.

There were things she couldn't describe, things she would never know. Richie was all but lost to them now, almost always unreachable, surfacing back in Waterford just once for Christmas in 1993 and then disappearing again. She could not speak enough to take up the absences of others, but she could recite her own sort of prayers to fill the space of her former silences, she could provide room for her daughter to do the same.

In that space she hoped the lineaments of her original apology, so negligible in its merely spoken form, would become evident and concrete. The apology she could not voice eloquently, the one which would never end and which she pushed toward Lucy and the girl whose life she had taken, and toward herself, each morning that she woke, thinking I'm sorry, I'm sorry, I'm sorry. Thinking the mantra Richie had once told her he used to lull himself to sleep:

I'm a good person and other people think so too.

Acknowledgements

Thank you to my agent and friend Harriet Moore for again being a crucial champion of my work when I had no faith in it myself. My dazzling team at Jonathan Cape, especially Michal Shavit whose instincts about the pacing and priorities of the novel vastly improved it. All involved with the Sunday Times Young Writer of the Year Award and the London Library, my membership of which turned out to be key as I wrote this second novel, and to the Society of Authors for their support through the Betty Trask Award.

Thanks as ever to my family for their support and love, my mam and dad Jim and Sue, step-parents Ger and Trudi, and brothers Gavan and Luke and sister-in-law Lisa, and most especially my nephew Cillian.

Thank you to Mike Whiteside for your unwavering help and care and providing brightness and laughter when I was in the worst of it, I love you very much.

Much love and gratitude to Jean Garnett, Nick Kinsey and Zuzu and Dilly for hosting me in upstate New York while I did the last mad dash of writing this past autumn.

To my London/UK friends I saw lots of as I wrote this book: Doireann Larkin, Orit Gat, Emmie Francis, Crispin Best, Rachel Benson, Mat Riviere, Francisco Garcia, Stan Cross, Josh Baines, Charles Olafare, Thea Everett, Lolly Adefope, Heather Mackintosh, Rosa Lyster, John Phipps,

James Vincent, Cam Spence, Maddie Mortimer, Sophie Collins, Roy Claire Potter – yous make life worth living; thank you for the good times, they will never rot.

And my New York pals old and new: Orlando Fitzgerald, Menachem Kaiser, John Ganz, Julia DeBenedictis, Michael Quinn, Anika Jade, Charlie Baker, Dan Poppick, Kendall Storey, Sam Rutter, all of whom gamely entertained me as I paid increasingly manic visits to the city last year, and Hanna Halperin and Nicola Maye Goldberg for reading at the paperback launch so beautifully.

Peter Huhne – *quel plaisir*, darling.

Read on for a conversation
with Megan Nolan

What was your inspiration for *Ordinary Human Failings*?

In very direct terms it was inspired by a short reference in the Gordon Burn non-fiction book *Somebody's Husband, Somebody's Son*, which is about Peter Sutcliffe, the serial killer who terrorised the north of England in the 1970s and 80s. Burn recounts that a tabloid approached some members of Sutcliffe's family once he had been arrested and offered to put them up in a hotel and give them booze and money in exchange for being an exclusive source, divulging dark details about the murderer. I may be misremembering this, because I deliberately never went back to check the details once I began to write. I didn't want to be influenced by specifics or indeed to be disheartened to discover I had gotten it entirely wrong and the premise never existed as it did in my mind.

Regardless, this idea of a hotel and a family kept contained by a journalist with ill intentions toward them seemed an irresistibly neat structure from which to explore a family, which is what I always really want to do with fiction. I began to contemplate who they were, what crime brought them to this explosive point, and how a child might become capable of such a thing. By the time I was writing the novel, we were in the second lockdown of the pandemic and I was living alone in London, feeling very lonely and far from my family. Writing a Waterford family was some comfort while I missed my own. Although the Greens could not be more divergent from my family, to imagine them walking our streets and estates felt soothing.

What appeals to you about family stories? You present a nuanced, multi-layered portrait of the Greens. What did you want to explore through them?

I've always loved more than anything to read a satisfying, intimate family portrayal in fiction. From *The Hotel New Hampshire* by John Irving to *The Gathering* by Anne Enright to *The Love Songs of W.E.B. Du Bois* by Honorée Fanonne Jeffers, many of my most cherished reading experiences have been with families. I think partly this is because of the exclusion inherent in the typical nuclear family unit. The premise of 'the family' as a concept, such as it exists in our culture, is that it is self-prioritising. It protects its survival and continuance by hiding the complex reality from outside view. The jovial, comfortable presentation of any family which is not our own, no matter how well adjusted or well off they may be, conceals any number of dynamics we can only guess at, and I've always found this fascinating – and frustrating! I'm nosy, I want to steal glimpses at all these private worlds I will never know. Creating my family, the Greens, was one way to address that instinct to unveil such privacy. The format of the novel involves multiple external perspectives on the family – neighbours, teachers, police, journalist – before swooping in and excavating their interiority and hidden selves. That felt very exciting to me.

Carmel's youth is full of possibility, but by her adulthood this freedom has been lost. What do you hope readers will reflect on after encountering her life?

The part of inequality, economic and otherwise, that I find most tragic is that second chances are not doled out the same to everyone who makes a mistake. A person with great means may make any number of mistakes but be able to recover from them well enough to begin again. A person with limited means, whether financial or emotional, may make one and never recover from it. The Greens aren't abjectly poor, but they are not well off and they are emotionally crippled for the various reasons we learn through their histories. One thing I wanted to explore within their story was the way in which mistakes of equal gravity can be so differently expressed in one life compared to another. Carmel's unwanted teenage pregnancy was an unfortunate turn of events, certainly, but many people recover from this experience, whether by having access to abortion or by feeling the support and confidence to raise a child and attempt to regroup and build a different life than the one which was previously imagined. Carmel has limited financial resources but, more crucially, despite being bold and confident in some ways, she has limited emotional resources from the subdued atmosphere of shared repression she grew up within. She cannot recover from this incident, and as somebody with a personal history with abortion in Ireland before it was legalised in 2018, that coin-flip of who gets to move on and who doesn't was very meaningful for me to interrogate.

There are two dominant characters: Carmel and the journalist Tom Hargreaves. Did you begin with one voice or did you always intend to offer multiple perspectives?

I always imagined the book as a chorus of the family members and Tom, but I wasn't initially sure how weighted each character would be. For instance, I began the book with Tom, and in the first draft there was substantially more material in Tom's voice, perhaps 10,000 words or so. Eventually these were excised or drastically edited down, because my wonderful editor Michal Shavit and I agreed that the Green family was the real heart of the book and that Tom's voice being as present as theirs felt a little off somehow. Then there was the question of which family members to involve and for how long. Rose had her own section at first, but it quickly became clear that the present-day action of the hotel was the clarifying moment which would be used to reveal the buried family dynamics, and as Rose is by this point dead, it felt unnatural to host her perspective so fully. There was also the question of whether to probe Lucy's interiority more actively, but fiction written from a child's perspective is incredibly hard to pull off, and also the mystery of how much she knows, sees and feels is crucial to the mystery of the book, so I decided to wait until later in the flash forward to her life as a teenager to really try to do that.

Carmel eventually returns to Waterford from London and we learn that every so often 'the feeling of being a family, which she had not felt since she was a child, came back'. Can we talk about what has allowed this change for her? Is being back in Ireland significant?

I think for her there is something profound and atavistic about not just Ireland but the family home on Mayor's Walk itself. It's something I've been thinking about a lot lately as a quite nomadic person. I try to assure myself that my surroundings aren't crucial, that I have myself and my work and people I love. There is a Jeanette Winterson quote from *Why Be Happy When You Could Be Normal?* which means a lot to me, where she refers to living in short-term chaotic situations as a young person and carrying a small rug with her to each place, her only constant – this constant reminds her that she has herself, which is enough to survive. I do believe in that, and yet what I feel when I return to Waterford is specific, an ancient feeling, not replicable anywhere else on earth. Like Carmel, I can feel my family there, even those who aren't alive or present. And there is something about getting older, less restless and unsatisfiable, which makes you value the anchor of the home place and the people who raised you in it where it once felt stifling.

The final sentence of *Ordinary Human Failings* is 'I'm a good person and other people think so too'. Can you share a little on your exploration of morality in the book?

I think the older I get the more intensely mortified I am at realising how much suffering surrounds us and how ignorant we can be about it. That's necessary in a way as we can't go through life agonising over the troubles of each person we encounter, but even the most basic building blocks of existence, the most typical and undramatic kind – birth and death and love and grief – are such vast forces that sometimes it amazes me that any of us function at all. It's painful to realise these things but I suppose in an ideal world we would accept that pain as fully as possible and try to use it to understand others better, even those we hate, who have hurt us, who do terrible things.

Which writers and books have influenced you the most?

Admittedly my earliest and therefore most important literary influences are a pretty homogenous group – white American men. At around thirteen, when I was getting serious about reading and writing, I loved *The Corrections* by Jonathan Franzen, *American Psycho* by Bret Easton Ellis, *The Virgin Suicides* by Jeffrey Eugenides and *The World According to Garp* by John Irving. They kickstarted things and then I branched out a little, but I can't deny those books caused me to want to be a novelist. I loved poetry too, devoured Adrienne Rich and W. D. Snodgrass and Frank O'Hara. Later into my writing life, I found my earnest yearning – sometimes poetic, sometimes just funny and pathetic – was richly rewarded reading *Giovanni's Room* by James Baldwin, *I Love Dick* by Chris Kraus, *A Man in Love* by Karl Ove Knausgaard. When I'm stuck on something, to this day sometimes I'll write out by hand my favourite sentences by Denis Johnson and Georges Bataille for the sheer exhilarating kick of them.

penguin.co.uk/vintage